MW01520043

THE RAZORBLADES IN MY HEAD

DONNIE GOODMAN

Copyright © 2021 by Donnie Goodman

All rights reserved.

No part of this book may be reproduced in any form or by any electronic or mechanical means, including information storage and retrieval systems, without written permission from the author, except for the use of brief quotations in a book review.

First Edition

The stories included in this collection are works of fiction. Names, characters, places and incidents are products of the author's imagination or are used fictitiously. Any resemblance to actual events or locales or persons living or dead is entirely coincidental.

Cover Art: Justin T. Coons

Content Warning: this collection features a number of scenes, scenarios, and descriptions that could potentially cause emotional distress.

PRAISE FOR DONNIE GOODMAN

"If this is only the beginning of his career, I look forward to watching how much better he gets. Goodman has a bright future ahead of him."

WESLEY SOUTHARD, SPLATTERPUNK AWARD-WINNING AUTHOR OF CRUEL SUMMER AND RESISTING MADNESS

"Unashamedly gleeful and wholeheartedly enjoyable The Old Bay King is the perfect read for a horror fan looking for a quick piece of pure horror gratification."

RICHARD MARTIN, MYINDIEMUSE.COM

"Hats off to Donnie Goodman for writing something that can go toe to toe with Brian Keene."

JORDAN ANDERSON, GOODREADS

For Meg

CONTENTS

The Razorblades in my Head 1

Third Grade 9

Stargazing 13

Gobble, Gobble 24

Magic in the Hat 29

It's Not Always Why 43

The Stranger in the Squared Circle 52

Toasted 77

Teddy 80

A Bloody Heist 91

Hourglass 98

The Old Bay King 104

Acknowledgments 125

Razorblade Notes 127

About the Author 139

"A good picture, any picture, has to be bristling with razorblades."

PABLO PICASSO

THE RAZORBLADES IN MY HEAD

I could feel it growing on my scalp. A little painful bump hiding underneath the oily mane of my brown hair. I found it one morning while shampooing my head before work. Even though I knew it wasn't a good idea, I caught myself running my fingers across the growth every ten to fifteen minutes. I couldn't help myself.

I thought it was acne.

Given the chance, I wouldn't wish cystic acne upon anyone, even my worst enemy on this God forsaken planet. My skin cleared up in my late 20's, but to this day I can't look at people in their eyes. Back when my face was covered with open sores, I figured if I stared at the ground during a conversation the zits would disappear. I still walk past mirrors expecting to find my face riddled with the pus-filled lesions that once made children in my presence shudder.

Believe me, I tried every product that they marketed during the commercial breaks on MTV, but to be clear, Clearasil wasn't going to help me out. By the time I turned sixteen, I was on a heavy regimen of prescription strength benzoyl peroxide, tretinoin cream, and accutane. That drug caused another kid my age to crash a single pilot Cessna into a building only three months after 9/11.

"What's that red stuff?" A neighbor's four year old once asked me while I shot a basketball on the patio of my backyard. I didn't know what to say, so I ignored him and kept on dribbling.

Denial is a hell of a tool and mine is wicked sharp.

It was hard to deny the fists to the stomach I took while changing in the locker room before gym class.

"You fat, fucking faggot," Bruce would say, laughing as he rifled through my belongings. "Why don't you stop drinking so much soda? You'd be less fat and your face wouldn't look like you've sucked on a bunch of herpes infected dicks." I'd laugh along with him like I was in on the joke.

Locker room talk, right?

I've been told that if you experience something often enough, you'll get used to it. Somehow, I got used to the way Bruce treated me throughout high school. The beatings, the name calling, the rumors he spread about me. The first time I ever went to a party he drugged my beer, stripped me while I was passed out, and took pictures of me lying naked in a bathtub. The polaroids were taped up throughout the school hallways the following Monday for hours before administrators finally took them down. All of that, I got used to. But I never got used to the acne.

I apply concealer on my face every day even though it's clear now. I deal with razor burn on occasion, but that's it. If you look close you can see scars on my cheeks, but I hide most of them with a beard. By the time I hit my thirties I had forgotten most things about my past. The real world caught up with me. I found plenty of other things to worry about.

Then, I felt the bump.

I snuck into the bathroom during my shift waiting tables to try and get a close look at it with my makeup mirror. Sure enough, when I parted my hair I found it dead center on the back of my head: a red bump about the size of a pen point. I had learned over time to leave zits alone and let them run their course, but I made the mistake of squeezing it. This sent a jolt of pain radiating throughout my body like I had never experienced. It was so bad I nearly blacked out and collapsed onto the tile floor for a few seconds, my vision blotting like those paintings they show you at the shrink.

I got up and went back to serving and completed my shift, but I could feel it throbbing, pulsing to the beat of my anxious heart. As soon as I got home, I ran to my bathroom mirror. Now the bump was the size of a dime and crusted over with a yellow scab that was rough to the touch. For the first time in years I anxiously tried searching WebMD for tips on how to deal with acne, but for some reason my internet was down. So I called to set up a repair appointment and applied some generic salicylic acid cream I had in my medicine cabinet on the spot before going to bed. That night I could feel myself messing with it even though I was dead asleep.

In my dreams, I saw a figure. A reflection of myself surrounded by a hollow darkness.

"Scars are not a sign of where we have healed, they are a reminder of what we have buried beneath the skin," it said to me.

"What do you mean?" I could hear myself ask. The figure reached out to me with its cold, dark hand.

"It is time to dig," it said.

I woke up, feverish, in a cold sweat. I ran to the bathroom and nearly tripped over a pile of laundry, but I had to see the bump again. When I held up the pocket mirror behind my head while facing the larger bathroom mirror, I screamed. The bump was now a full inch in diameter and protruding about a quarter inch off of my skull. It was a variety of colors: reds, whites, and yellows. I got some gauze, hydrogen perox- ide, and a washcloth while I prepared some hot water so I could try to compress the growth into submission. I hoped it would pop easily, allowing the healing process to begin.

When I pressed into it with the washcloth I was hit with a strange sensation. There was something hard and pointy in the middle of the growth. I dropped the cloth and placed my right pointer finger on the hard point and pushed down. The bump gave way to something metallic and I heard it burst. I also felt a tremendous jolt of pain. I looked down to see that the tip of my finger had been sliced down the middle leaving two equal folds of skin which gushed blood onto the floor. I felt sick. I wrapped my finger with the gauze and medical tape before staring in disbelief into the mirror.

The thing I had assumed was a growing zit had given birth to a steel razorblade. Half of it was still wedged tightly into my head. I started crying. My right hand hurt so bad that I had to reach around with my left in order to confirm what I was seeing was accurate.

It wasn't my imagination.

I pinched my fingers together on the flat metal surface of the blade. I pulled slightly, but there was absolutely no give to it. At this point, I probably should have called 911, but I was in shock. My only thought was *I need to get this fucking razor out of my skull,* so I grabbed a set of pliers and got to work. I tugged as hard as I could as pus, blood, and clear bodily fluids dripped into my sink. The pliers slipped off the edge of the blade and the momentum of the pull brought my jaw crashing down on the sink's hard ceramic edge.

I woke up lying on my bathroom floor to the sound of someone knocking on my door. I took a look in the mirror and ran my fingers through my hair and to my horror, I could now feel dozens of similar bumps all over my head. The knocking continued. I frantically put on a snapback and opened the door to find the internet repair guy standing there.

"You ok, bud?" he asked. I realized that I was covered in dried blood and other gross fluids and my finger was still wrapped tightly in bandages. When we made eye contact, I felt my heart race. I moved to the side so he could enter. I stood there choking on my words as he casually approached the living room.

"I just need you to show me where your router is. I've brought a replacement. We've been upgrading them throughout the area the past few weeks as these older models are phased out..." he stopped talking. I think he had grown uncomfortable by the way I smiled at him. I looked over his shoulder and the dark reflection from my dream was standing there smiling back at me. I could feel the bumps growing larger by the second.

I took my hat off.

"Your, your head," he said stumbling backwards, but it was too late. I shut the door and locked the dead bolt.

"What are you doing?"

I closed the distance between us in three quick steps and pushed him into the wall as hard as I could. The dark figure clapped in delight. Then, I head butted him in the face. The thick part of my forehead cracked into the bridge of his nose, shattering it. I pushed him onto the floor and he lay there screaming in pain. His nostrils bled as I lifted up his work shirt to expose his bare chest. The shirt was patched with a name tag that read: Bruce.

I laughed so hard it made me realize I hadn't belted out real ones in years.

It felt nice.

I was overcome with a desperate need for release, the same feeling you get before a sneeze or a huge orgasm, when something odd happened. The razorblades in my head came exploding out of my skull. Some of them hit the ceiling, some of them hit the wall in front of us, and some of them remained sticking out of my head, glimmering in the sunlight that pierced my living room window. I straddled the man who once tortured me relentlessly. A man who no longer had any idea who I was.

"One thing about me, Bruce, is I never forget a face," I said before bringing my head down into his stomach. I could hear the blades puncture his organs and felt the warmth of his guts, which spilled onto the floor of my house. I brought my head down repeatedly in a series of wet thuds that sent splashes of blood across the vanilla walls of my living room. I worked my head down his arms and legs, carving deep lines into the skin. He spasmed for a minute or two and then he stopped moving. Satisfied, I lay there for a few minutes catching my breath.

"No longer buried," the figure said, reaching out to me once again. We walked hand in hand to my tool shed where I grabbed a shovel. In the reflection of the stainless steel shovel head, I could see that the empty holes in my skull had already started to fade away.

"It is time to dig," I said.

THIRD GRADE

I'm trying to get smarter Mrs. Bender.

I promise.

I didn't remember to do my homework yesterday because when I got home from school I forgot all about it. I drew in my notebook all night long. I'm making a video game called "Terror Team." It's a lot like Mega Man 5, but even harder. I would bring in my level drawings to show you, but Jamie threw my notebook away in the cafeteria trash can. I had to start all over again because he got chocolate milk all over it and now it is wrinkled and it smells horrible.

I hate Jamie.

Why didn't he get in trouble when he sat on Berries and killed her? He said it was an accident but I think he did it on purpose.

I miss Berries.

I drew a picture of her running around the classroom in her little plastic ball. I should have been working on my book report. I wanted to do Pet Sematary, but Principal Turner said I'm not allowed to read Stephen King books anymore. I think it's because you caught me digging in the trash can to try and find Berries. I just wanted to bring her home with me even though she was flat like the pizza they make us eat on Wednesdays, the ones with the little weird pepperoni pieces on them. Mom and Dad told me I can read whatever I want. I'm writing my own book called "Blood Beach 2." It's a lot like Jaws, but even scarier.

I've been working really hard on making 30 free throws in a row. Right now I can only get to 17 or 18.

Mr. Morris has cerebral palsy so he can only shoot with one hand and he can only walk on one foot, but I've seen him make 50 in a row. He told me to keep trying.

I'm sorry I talk with Alex too much.

Alex is my best friend.

I'm sad he has to move back to Maine this summer. His parents are mad at him because they found his box with the weird pictures in them. Everyone in them is wearing black clothes and is naked and tied up and they look afraid. Alex told me that his older brother gave them to him. His brother told him not to tell anyone about it. I probably shouldn't have told you.

We want to come up with the perfect band name. I haven't learned how to play guitar yet, but Alex's brother has a drum set. We want to play like Nirvana, but even louder. Alex is writing a song called "Raisin Bladders."

I am worried about the test next week.

I can't ever remember the last step in long division. My last teacher told me that I would never learn math because I'm always in the clouds and I should be on the ground.

I like clouds.

I know you are worried too, Mrs. Bender.

I am sorry your husband died over Winter Break.

I saw you take his picture off of your desk and cry during silent reading. It will be okay, Mrs. Bender. I would hold your hand if I could, but you moved my seat to the back row so that I wouldn't talk with Alex too much. Now, I can't see the board and I'm next to the big window so I can't focus on what you want me to learn. I look out the window all day long.

Last week, I got an idea Mrs. Bender.

I don't think your husband is buried in the right cemetery. If he had been, he would be home with you right now and you wouldn't need to cry ever again. I read in the newspaper that Harry is in Westmoreland Cemetery and I told Alex about it.

He got an idea too.

We rode our bikes to the cemetery over the week-end. We went with his brother and we brought some shovels and some crowbars with us. We dug and dug and dug. I swear we were going to reach the other side of the world, we dug for so long. But you told us to never give up, so we kept digging and digging and after a few hours, Alex's brother finally hit the coffin. We ripped a hole into it with the crowbars, but we couldn't move Harry's body because he was too heavy and the hole we dug was too deep. Alex said we should at least get the head since we did all that digging.

I think that's all you need, really.

After a few hits with the shovel, it came right off and we put it into my backpack. It doesn't smell very good, so I put it in a big zip lock bag and sprayed it with some Lysol.

I know that if you bury this in the right place, Harry will come back and you can be together again just like me and Alex. He told me that one day he will move back here from Maine and we will be able to play our songs.

I'll leave my backpack under your desk when we go out for recess Mrs. Bender. I know you'll find Harry's head and know exactly what to do with it. It won't get thrown away like Berries.

I'm gonna chase Julia today during tag.

STARGAZING

It is 3:07 a.m. when Imani gets the first text.

Deep in between REM cycles, she sleeps through it.

She walks through a shallow creek bed while her brother sifts through a pile of small rocks, mud, and detritus. They're looking for jewels. She listens to the pieces of earth colliding into each other over the constant rush of a stream somewhere along the New River. Her father, donned in a camouflaged hoodie and Virginia Tech hat, pulls a fishing net through the water downstream, hoping to catch some crawfish to boil for dinner. They make eye contact and he winks at her, lovingly.

"Look Imani, I found something!" her brother, Malik, says with a level of excitement only possessed by six year old boys. She looks over from the opposite side of the water to see a small, beautiful mineral nestled in the palms of his tiny hands. It is two inches in diameter and veined with a seemingly infinite network of deep blue crystals.

"That is one pretty chunk of Kyanite," she says.

"Ky-uh-nite," he repeats back to her, laughing.

Her little brother is notorious for keeping his eyes on the ground, while Imani has a reputation for pointing her eyes to the heavens.

Mama calls her Stargazer.

She admires Malik for his stubborn will and fierce determination. She wades over to give him a celebratory hug, when the stream suddenly separates into a pitch black chasm. A smell of decay and rot fills the air, so thick, she can see it, along with the sinkhole that swallows Malik. She has no time to warn him. The skin of his face dissolves, leaving behind a pale, white skull. He lifts his skeletal hands up in a final move of desperation. Then, he disappears into oblivion.

Her lungs fill with water.

Buzz.

Buzz, Buzz.

Imani wakes in a cold sweat, confused, as the glow of her smartphone display ticks on and off in a steady, but uncoordinated rhythm of notifications. She looks over at the alarm clock on her bedside table which reads 4:36 am. She sighs, burying her face back into the pillow. All Imani wants right now is to fall back asleep for a few more hours before her 12 hour shift at the Verbena Hospital begins, but she makes the same mistake she has told herself not to make countless times, on countless nights, before this one: she decides to check her phone.

She looks into the camera and unlocks it.

Shelly: The lights are beautiful.
Shelly: I've never seen anything like this in my whole life.
Derek: This is incredible!
Mama: I see them. I see Malik.
Brad: Did you look?

Her messenger inbox is filled with notifications indicating new messages. Some of them are from close friends and relatives, but many of them are from people who somehow made it into her contact list over the years, but have not spoken to her in any context that she can remember at this point in her life.

"Who the hell is Brad?" she says, while rolling over onto her side. She is still half trapped in the nightmare which pulled her back into consciousness. She remembers, as she does every single morning, that Malik is gone.

Malik is dead.

She replies to Mama: Mama, that's not funny.

She replies to her best friend, Shelly: Lol, what are you talking about?

Imani is hit with an unquenchable thirst. The need is so strong that she doesn't even attempt to make it to the kitchen of her duplex to get water from her fridge. She heads into the bathroom and puts an empty plastic bottle up to the sink faucet, filling it to the top with lukewarm water. She gulps the entire thing down without taking a breath.

From the darkness of her bedroom, she can see the phone lighting up once again like a firefly searching for a mate. She shuffles back to the device, expecting a response from Mama or Shelly, but this is not what she finds. Her phone continues pinging message alerts from unknown numbers. First, a few, then a dozen, and then, what seems like hundreds.

571-457-1367: I will never forget this.

540-331-2987: Revelation 21:4

540-331-2987: He will wipe away every tear from their eyes

540-331-2987: and death shall be no more

540-331-2987: neither shall there be mourning

540-331-2987: nor crying nor pain any more

540-331-2987: for the former things have passed away

540-331-2987: Pray for me

804-295-2237: I found them

319-771-8989: I never believed I was ready until now.

Imani scans through a few of the messages before tossing the phone down onto the comforter on her bed. She is scared. It doesn't take but a few seconds before she picks the phone back up and presses the Twitter icon, but her profile and timeline do not load. She pulls her finger down across the screen a few more times to try and refresh the feed, but all she gets is an error message. She repeats this process with a few other social networks, but nothing seems to work at the moment. As her finger hovers over the Safari browser icon, a sharp tone rings out and she jumps up, startled. Another text alert pops up on her phone:

Presidential Alert: This is NOT a test.
All citizens of the United States, shelter in place.
If you are outside, seek shelter immediately.

What the fuck is going on, she thinks. Working a long shift at the nursing clinic is no longer a concern. Pacing in a small circle in her bedroom, she turns on her bedside lamp and grabs the remote to her television. She ditched cable years ago, but she has a hacked Chromecast which should be able to pull up CNN. She hopes that Don Lemon will help her figure out exactly what is happening.

There is a noise.

It is not exactly a sound, but a wave of vibrations that Imani feels pulse through her apartment. It starts in the front hallway of the duplex, moves through her body, and out through her bedroom window. The short hairs on her arms and neck stand up and in an instant, the image displayed on her TV powers off, her lights go out, and her smartphone is rendered into a black mirror, a useless brick.

In the pitch black, she carefully moves her hands across the wall until she reaches the light switch in her bedroom. She flips the switch up and down a few times, but nothing happens. She stumbles down the hallway of her apartment, eventually finding herself digging through a drawer filled with junk in her kitchen.

"Gotcha," she says, relieved, finding a yellow emergency flashlight she keeps stocked just for moments like this. She clicks the "on" button a few times, but the flashlight is unresponsive. It slowly dawns on Imani that every single item in her house that is powered by electricity is dead. It doesn't matter if it is powered by an outlet, or powered by batteries.

If it has a circuit board, it is dead.

She notices how quiet the room is. It is eerie. The creaking of the ceiling fan, the slight hum of her fridge, the buzzing of her central air system. It has never been this quiet in her place. She closes her eyes to help focus her ears on the various noises emanating from outside. She can't hear much, so she cracks open the kitchen window and immediately hears the sounds of dogs barking. Dozens of them. A chorus of labradors and hounds, howling, snarling, and shrieking with fear into the strange night. Then, there is the unmistakable sound of a large aircraft descending rapidly in the air, followed by a concussive explosion somewhere far off in the distance.

The silence returns.

"Oh my God," Imani says, her chest heaving up and down in rapid, anxious breaths. She inhales, deeply, while counting down from 200. While this technique for managing anxiety usually works when she is in a crowded supermarket, or dealing with a tough patient, it isn't helping much right now.

"Snap the fuck out of it," she tells herself.

She remembers she has a box of strike anywhere matches and some candles underneath the sink, so she kneels down to the cabinet doors and finds them while attempting to fight off an unrelenting sense of panic. Her hands shake so badly that she fails to strike the match against the tile floor successfully on the first try. She fails again on the second try. On her third strike, the match lights.

There is a man in her kitchen.

Imani screams as the man puts up his hands in a gesture of peace. The breath of air extinguishes the match. They are once again surrounded by total darkness.

"I'm sorry, Imani. I didn't mean to startle you. Your door was unlocked," the man says.

Imani drops the box of matches on the floor and puts her hands up to her face. She sobs in relief. She is so thankful that she recognized the voice.

"Mr. Walters, what are you doing here?" She asks her neighbor from down the block. Imani frequently babysat his children before they entered junior high and she completed nursing school. She remembers the many times he helped jump her piece of shit car so she would not be late for work. She bends down, strikes another match, and lights a candle.

"They're gone," he says.

"Who's gone?" Imani asks, holding up the candle so that she can get a good look at his face. Mr. Walters has an expression that she cannot easily classify. The emotions radiating from his wide eyes are crazed and his lips are trembling with the vibrato of a high pitched scream, but he does not make a noise. It is a look that she has never seen on anyone before. Tears spill from his eyes and slide down his cheeks. It is so quiet she can hear the droplets splash on to the floor.

"Everyone," he says.

Imani is about to ask him what he means by that, when he pulls a black 9mm handgun out of the back pocket of his bluejeans. She doesn't have any time to react before he puts the gun up to his right temple and pulls the trigger. The gunshot is so loud, Imani is still focusing on regaining her hearing before she notices that small, sharp fragments of Mr. Walters' skull are embedded into the sides of her face. He slumps over and falls to the floor, his head cracking on the tile. Imani vomits. The bottle of water comes shooting back out of her throat mixed with bile and Mr. Walters' blood, bone, and brain matter.

She can no longer process what is taking place. She is in shock. A weird sense of calm washes over her body in a series of waves as she walks to the front door of her apartment.   She unlatches the deadbolt and opens the door. In the distance, she can see an orange glow from a structure fire, probably caused by the plane that fell from the sky. She scans the area left to right and catches sight of her neighbor from across the street, Jose.   He moved into the neighborhood a few years ago after immigrating from Honduras.   His Chevy Silverado is parked in the middle of the street. It appears the engine died before he was able to pull into the driveway. Jose stands in the bed of the truck, balanced on top of a contractors ladder rack. He is looking up at the sky.

A blueish beam of light shines down on Jose. She can see that he is smiling. She watches in horror as Jose's feet begin to disappear. He is still standing there on the ladder, but it appears as if each atom of his body is slowly being stripped away, subatomic bit by subatomic bit. It starts at his feet, then his hands, and she watches as his skin, muscles, and bones vanish into a thin trail of dust. The particles are sucked upwards as if being pulled in by some sort of vacuum. Even though it feels like an eternity, it doesn't take long.

Jose is gone.

Imani wants to leave. She wants to head back into her home, lock the door, and hide in her bedroom closet. If she goes back to sleep right now, maybe she will wake up again and this second nightmare will be over too.

Then, she hears his voice.

"Look, Imani, I found something."

Malik is standing in the grass, five yards away, holding a piece of Kyanite. She knows this isn't real, because she once had to learn how leukemia, in fact, is. She watched the disease slowly and methodically destroy her little brother from the inside out, a brother that she loved dearly. She grabs her necklace, the chunk of Kyanite Malik once found in the creek bed of their home in Blacksburg, Virginia. She squeezes it tightly, crying out loud. She just wants to give him a hug. Malik smiles at her as she steps outside past the threshold of the apartment.

"It's ok to look up," he says.

There is something deep within Imani which tells her not to. She isn't stupid. She knows how dangerous it could be. She has never felt fear the way she currently does, but at the end of the day, she is human and she can't help it.

She looks up.

There, in the sky, is a black orb that stretches past the viewable horizon of the night. The object is so enormous it blocks her view of the full moon. Even in the pitch black darkness, she can somehow see it. Its metallic surface reflects a sinister intelligence that seeps into her consciousness. The orb floats, suspended in the atmosphere, hovering silently. She cannot breathe. She cannot even begin to understand it. As she scans the surface of the orb, she sees millions of individual beams of light, piercing into the earth at various angles. The Kyanite around her neck begins to pulse, warmly. A beam of light settles on her and she knows that Malik is no longer standing there. He was never standing there.

Imani thinks about the meaningless stack of utility bills sitting on her kitchen table, the collection agency still trying to track down the medical debt her family owes. Her student loan, which is in default. She thinks about every stupid argument she ever had with her dad and how she stopped answering his calls after she graduated from college. She regrets not going to his funeral when he hung himself in the garage of their childhood home.

She looks down.

Her feet begin to pull apart into tiny strands of matter. She feels each protein being separated and pulled upwards into the orb.

It hurts.

She used to find peace in the infinite possibilities that the stars represented when she was a child, but the orb has blocked the sky. The orb is the only thing she can see as she dematerializes.

Mama called her Stargazer.

GOBBLE, GOBBLE

Garth Miller wasn't good at damn near anything in this life if it didn't involve killing turkeys. He picked up the trade from his Pa, like his Pa had picked it up from his Pa, and even though the Gainer Corp. purchased the family slaughterhouse back in the spring of 86', Garth took great pride and enjoyment in his duties. He cleared the trucks of all the birds who died of hypothermia and dehydration. He shackled legs. He slit throats. But his favorite thing was dropping them into the boiler. Some of them, hell, many of them went in still alive and conscious, dozens at a time. He'd laugh and holler along with his crew as they processed 1500 turkeys an hour on some days, especially around Thanksgiving.

Today, it was the eve of this holiday and Garth was particularly excited to show up for work. It was bonus day and his crew had been efficient and productive over the past quarter. He joked with Clint, another gifted turkey processor, on the killing floor,

"I need that bonus *today*. I'm gonna get me a lap dance from Ruby Lips that lasts for a few songs. That's all I need. I've got my jerk off pants on underneath my kill coat and everything!"

"You're heading over there without going home and showering first. What the hell is wrong with you," Clint said. Garth laughed.

"I don't want any other man getting to Ruby first tonight. She's all mine."

He licked his lips and grabbed his crotch. Clint sprayed the remaining viscera into a large drain on the floor of the shed.

"Come on then Casanova, we have one more unit to knock out. We don't want to keep Ruby Lips waiting," he said, imagining the brutish oaf entering their local strip club smelling like turkey guts. The pair slid open the hatch of Building 12. This was the second largest processing station on the 150 acre property. Garth and Clint stopped dead in their tracks. Something wasn't right.

The turkeys were missing.

"What the hell is going on here, where is the lot?" He said. The pair looked inside, bewildered. The hundreds of hooks which normally held the fleshy, featherless carcasses swung empty throughout the shed. The long rows of sterile, fluorescent work lights had been cut off, so they couldn't see more than ten yards inside.

"Where the hell is Josue?" Clint asked. They began to walk inside, searching for clues as to what may have happened. Garth was not amused.

"I swear, if that fuck messes with my bonus I'm gonna tear him to pieces," he said, as Clint fumbled with a power switch. He moved a series of levers up and down, but nothing happened.

"I guess the power's out," he said.

"There's got to be a flashlight around here some-where, open that door and let some more sunlight in—"

His instruction was cut short by the lone call of a turkey somewhere within the darkness of the shed.

"Gobble," it said.

Garth had spent his entire life around the slaugh-terhouse. He only knew the turkey calls for fear and pain. This one was different. It was somehow, confi-dent. Knowing? He shook his head. Clint moved back inside before getting the chance to open the door.

"Come on out and let's see you, you ol' fat bird," Garth said. He grabbed a circular saw and revved it a few times while Clint flanked him. They moved into the musty darkness together.

"I don't like this one bit," Clint said.

"You're a grown man and you sound scared. It's pathetic."

Garth spit a wad of phlegm on to the stainless steel floor and revved his saw again. The pair moved halfway into the shed, when the lone call cried out from the darkness a second time.

"Gobble," it said, again.

This time, the utterance came from behind them, closer to the entrance. Clint whipped around in a panic.

"Shit, I need a saw," he said.

"Calm down, you'll be fine. I've been killing these fuckin' birds my whole life and they're all crown and no filling. Go get one from over there," he said, pointing to a large rectangular table that was near the entrance.

Clint took a step towards the table when they heard a strange commotion and a whooshing sound. Something darted past them. Garth felt a clump of feathers hit his lips along with the hot, unmistakeable taste of blood. Clint began to scream.

"Jesus, the damn thing bit my nose off!" he said, holding his face, mumbling incoherently. Clint broke for an escape, but he tripped and fell to the floor. It was the body of Josue, or what was left of him. Most of what was supposed to be inside his body was no longer there. He stared into an empty hole that ran from his neck down to his thighs.

Clint continued to scream while Garth swung his saw in a circular motion. He frantically attacked the darkness which enveloped them.

"I'm a Miller, you hear me?! A Miller! All we knows is how to use this here saw. Now come on out and do what you were born to do, so I can do what *I* was born to do."

Clint sobbed on the floor of the slaughterhouse as a crescendo of clicks circled around them. A volley of feathers swirled into the shape of a cyclone. The small sliver of sunlight which cut into the building gave them just enough visibility to perceive that the large flock of turkeys had prevented their escape. A beak ripped a gash into the web of flesh between Garth's thumb and pointer finger. He dropped the saw and fell to his knees. As he looked down, he saw pieces of Clint's face disappear in a horrible, nightmarish kaleidoscope. First his lips, then his cheeks, then his eyes. His skull was still screaming even as the birds devoured his face.

Garth had spent his entire life in this place and for the first time, he felt scared. He looked up towards the sky and began to say a prayer, but it was cut short as the birds closed in on him.

MAGIC IN THE HAT

They called themselves PKG.

Short for "Privileged Kids Gang,"every winter the trio of delinquents would raise hell up and down the cul-de-sacs of Greenfields, a gated community in the suburbs of Northern Virginia.

There was Cole, the leader, Jared, the muscle, and Brett, the wildcard. They viewed themselves as a legitimate criminal organization, but in reality they were just bored kids looking to pass the time while their parents were out of town or zonked out on anti-anxiety pills. They formed the posse when they were nine years old and what started as a harmless "boys only" club had escalated from all night video game sessions and contests to see who could drink the most Mountain Dew, into actual, real world crimes.

They keyed sports cars, egged the vacation homes of lawyers who lived in New York, and stole Amazon

Prime packages even though they never got anything good. They let air out of road bike tires, salted flower beds, and spray painted edgy phrases on local stop signs. Cole once added "jerkin it" on the red octagon nearest his house. He shared the pic he snapped of it on PKG's private Discord server. It took the HOA three full days before they finally removed it. He filmed the portly security guard out on a Saturday morning blasting the sign with a pressure washer. He could be overheard giggling in the background. That made it onto the discord too.

After four years of chaos, they had never been caught, much less suspected. They were privileged kids, after all. In school, the boys earned straight A's, played lacrosse, and went to church every Sunday. No one believed the vandalism and hijinks were coming from inside the community. In fact, the members of the Greenfields PTA petitioned the security department to start canvassing the nearby neighborhoods for suspects.

It was the winter of Cole's 13th birthday when a freak storm dropped 11 inches of snow across the mid-Atlantic region. With schools closed indefinitely, families spent their Monday mornings across the neighborhood sledding, clearing sidewalks, and making snowmen. By the middle of the afternoon, there were dozens of the sculptures scattered across the snow-blanketed lawns. Some were just lazily rolled together, but others got the full on Frosty treatment: adorned with carrot noses, charcoal eyes, scarves, and stick arms. In between PKG's usual rounds of Fortnite, Cole looked out of his bedroom window and got an idea.

A wonderfully awful idea.

As tradition dictated, he picked up his Motorola walkie talkie and sent out a call to action. The boys conducted all of their business this way. They had iPhones, but tradition was tradition.

"This is Captain Slaw, reporting live from the birdhouse. I repeat, this is Captain Slaw, reporting live from the birdhouse. Come in Young Slim, Come in. Over."

Brett, who lived directly across the street and was currently a team member in Cole's Fortnite squad joined in with an over the top pilot voice.

"Copy uhh. This is uhh, Young Slim uhh, go ahead there Captain Slaw. Over."

"I've got eyes on some Frostys that may need smashing. Over."

"Uhh copy that Slaw. Should I uhh, relay this to The Rock? Over."

Jared insisted that PKG call him "The Rock." As in, the WWE wrestler and actor. Jared was notorious in the 8th grade class. He hit puberty at 11, was already 6'2," and he could grow a full beard. Cole and Brett were honestly scared to say no, so he was known (although not affectionately) as "The Rock." Cole put his PS4 into standby mode and grinned. He looked up at his carefully positioned lacrosse stick, hanging on the wall of his bedroom above a collection of athletic trophies.

"Affirmative. Meet at the usual spot at the usual time. Over and out."

Tis the season for snowmen smashing, he thought.

PKG'S MISCHIEF always began in one place and at one time: The Greenfields tennis courts at 12:34 am. Cole arrived at midnight on the dot and sat waiting on a large pile of snow, pushed off the access road by the plow. Dressed in black Vans sneakers, black ski pants, a black North Face jacket and resting a black ski mask on the top of his head, he poured Coke into the snow next to him and scooped it into his mouth, fashioning a crude snow cone.

"Can I get one?" Brett asked, approaching from down the street. He was dressed in a similar fashion.

"I've got a yellow one just for you," Cole said, throwing a snowball in his direction. Brett shook his head and revealed his lacrosse stick. Flexing his non-existent muscles, he mimed the movements of The Incredible Hulk.

"I'm ready to SMASH," he said.

"I counted 25 on my way here."

"I'm sure there's more on Jared's street too. Speak of the devil."

Jared appeared in the direction opposite of Brett, a

large moving shadow that actually resembled the Hulk. He called out,

"Sorry y'all, I couldn't help myself so I got started on the way."

Cole wasn't pleased by this admission.

"What do you mean you already got started? You know the rules."

"I didn't smash anything" he said, holding up a small package in his sledgehammer sized hands.

"What is that?" Brett said.

"I don't know, I took it from the porch of a house on the way here."

Cole thought for a second, confused.

"They weren't making deliveries today Jared, the storm delayed shipping. I think all mail was routed to the main office."

"I don't know what you're talking about. I just saw it and took it like we always do. I brought it here so we could open it together."

The parcel was a small rectangular shape with no visible address and wrapped in dark, tan parchment paper. It was tied together with two pieces of twine that put out a surprisingly strong odor. It gave Brett the creeps.

"That doesn't look like mail," he said. Cole intervened.

"Whatever, let's open it," he said.

Jared handed him the package to let him do the honors. Cole ripped into it with the grace of a house cat stuck in a paper towel roll. Tearing away the paper revealed a small, black leather book.

"Great, a book. Let's go smash snowmen now," Brett said.

"No. Open it up," Jared said.

"I am," Cole said, making sure to emphasize that he was the leader and it was his idea to open the book. He flipped the cover open to a series of images the three boys wished they could unsee. The language on the first page wasn't written in English and it featured three diagrams of a man being gradually turned inside out. It didn't look like an anatomy drawing either, it just looked wrong. Cole tossed the book back at Jared.

"Where did you get this?" he asked.

"I don't know. It was from that house on Locust Street, the same one where we salted the herb garden last winter."

Brett took a puff from his inhaler and his expression became somber.

"My dad told me about that house recently. The guy who lives there is a hermit."

"He's a bird?" Jared asked.

"No you idiot, he doesn't leave the house," Cole said. Brett continued.

"Apparently his entire family died in the 80s in some tragic accident. They were killed by a drunk driver or something. No one knows anything about him other than he doesn't have kids, he's retired, and he used to run a circus when our parents were kids. And you stole his weird-ass book, Rock."

"Well if he doesn't leave the house, it's not like we have anything to worry about do we?" Jared said.

Cole shot him a piercing look and directed the group, pointing to an imaginary map with the end of his lacrosse stick.

"No, here's the plan. We came out tonight to smash snowmen and that is what we're going to do. Brett, you hit Cherry Street and Poplar Avenue. Jared, take this book back to that house and hit Locust Avenue and Arch Street. I'll knock out Spruce Street and Pine Street. Then we'll meet back here before heading to my place. I don't want to ever mention this book again. We're smarter than this. Take care of it, Rock."

"You all need to relax. I've got this." Jared said.

And with that, PKG split up to continue their night of misbehavior.

SQUISH.

Jared brought his size 12 boot down on a small snowman in the yard of a two story "Model C" home, the first in a group of three. He muttered to himself while he destroyed the work of the Williams Family.

"He thinks he knows everything," he said, kicking the head off of the next one. Jared was well aware he was bigger, stronger, and just as capable as Cole, but he couldn't bring himself to try and shift the power dynamics in PKG. Since his growth spurt, he had started to resent himself for his lack of defiance in the face of Cole's obnoxious adherence to rules they made when they were nine years old.

"It's not going to be this way forever," he grunted.

Jared worked his way down Locust Avenue, smashing snowmen until he arrived where the mysterious old hermit lived. The large home was a "Model B," completely indistinguishable from any of the other Model B's in Greenfields apart from an archaic doorknob that had been installed on the front door. The bronze fixture depicted a beast of some kind with open jaws in the process of swallowing the Earth. Its clawed feet held the knocker. It stood out in stark contrast to the "Live, Laugh, Love" sign Jared's parents had placed on their front door. The doorknob was clearly breaking HOA regulations, but after looking at that book he stole, he figured the HOA probably left the old man alone for good reasons.

He slowly walked up to the porch and dropped the book on the third step where it had previously caught his eye, but as he was about to turn and head back toward Arch Street, he was hit with an indescribably hostile urge to rap the knocker and then run away.

It's been at least two years since our last ding dong ditch game, he thought.

At 13, Jared's impulse control was non-existent, so he continued on up to the porch, grabbed the legs of the beast, and brought it down once with a force so strong he was worried it might have broken the knocker. The crack ricocheted off the porch ceiling and echoed down the street.

Jared turned to run, filled with energy from the adrenaline rush, but he never made it off the porch. A blunt object pierced his chest and pushed him up, off his feet. He looked down, befuddled by what he saw and felt. He was suspended in mid-air, his feet twitching six inches off the ground. A tree branch had pierced his chest, impaled him through his ribcage and exited from his back. He felt a chill move throughout his body as he lost consciousness.

BRETT WORKED his way down Cherry Street, thinking about the first time The PKG had a sleepover. They had spent the entire night watching Marvel movies, pretending to be The Avengers. Cole was Captain America, naturally. Jared was Iron Man, and Brett was The Incredible Hulk, ironically. Brett was always rail thin and now that he had started to notice girls in his class, he was self-conscious about his spindly frame. He adopted the nickname Young Slim as a joke, but quickly regretted it when he realized Cole and Jared called him that with almost a mocking tone.

The boys had taken a blood oath to be best friends forever, but with every passing year, Brett felt like that it was an empty promise. In his free time, he started collecting Warhammer figurines, but he kept the interest hidden from PKG. He just figured they'd make fun of him. In many ways, he missed the days where they just played like The Avengers. But tradition was tradition, so he smashed, and he smashed.

Halfway down Cherry Street, Brett brought his lacrosse stick high above his head in order to destroy a magnificent snowman the Rosenbergs had created, when he heard a scraping sound close behind him.

He stopped and turned his head to look back but saw nothing in the street behind him apart from a snowman where he had just finished smashing. Confused, he did a double take.

"Hello?" He said.

Nothing returned his call. I swear I already took care of that house, he thought.

"I guess I missed you," he said, preparing to strike with his lacrosse stick. He went to bring it up but felt a strange pull of resistance. He turned back toward the Rosenberg's snowman, which was now somehow holding on to the net with its stick arms.

"What the fuck," he said, pulling as hard as he could. With as much strength as he could muster, he pulled the stick away from the snowman, but slipped and fell into the street. As he hit the ground, he looked back. Now four snowmen waited in the yard where he had already smashed everything. He began to panic, and he did the only thing he could think to do.

He cried out for Cole.

IT WAS 1:40 a.m. when Cole started to worry. He had worked quickly through his allotment of snowmen. The families of Pine and Spruce Streets would wake up in the morning and find their source of enjoyment gone, and nothing made Cole happier. Currently, he felt annoyed. Maybe that lumbering asshole Jared got caught by Greenfield's security, he thought. Texting them at this point was too risky. If their parents saw them communicating this late, they may grow suspicious. He had given PKG enough time to meet back up, so he figured he would run recon on their potentially failed mission and then head back home.

He began by moving through Brett's route and while he couldn't find his friend, the snowmen had all been smashed, which was good. He knew he could count on Young Slim. Next, he worked his way down Arch Street and found his way to Locust Avenue. The results were the same.

No snowmen, no Jared.

He was just about to head home, when he decided to check up on Jared's other task.

"Let's see if he dropped off the book," he said, walking towards the old man's house.

He had ridden his bike past this house nearly his entire life and never stopped to think what kind of weirdo might be living inside it. In his mind, every adult in Greenfields was a lamb and he was the wolf.

As he approached the porch, he did not see the book anywhere.

"Goddammit Jared," he said.

It was at that moment when he heard a whimpering cry from the darkness in the backyard.

"Who's there?" he asked, pulling his lacrosse stick up into a defensive position. The whimpering continued. It was a muffled sound, like someone trying to speak with a hand over their face. He pulled out his cell phone, turned on the flashlight, and began moving towards the sound. As he rounded the corner of the house, he began to hear a chorus of things rolling towards him. It was a wet, crunchy roar. As he brought up his light, Cole realized that he was not a wolf, he was the lamb.

Brett stood in the backyard, but it was no longer Brett. His legs and torso had been replaced by mounds of snow that were visibly eating into the rest of his body. His neck was fused onto the monstrous mound, and it appeared, however impossible, that he was literally turning into a snowman. Next to Brett stood a snowman that was unmistakably large.

"Jesus," he said, turning to run.

He then realized that the rolling sound was coming from dozens of snowmen gathering at the house, seemingly from all across the Greenfields community. They formed a circle around him. Some of them had lifeless charcoal eyes, some of them held out their stick hands in a menacing gesture, some of them just sat there, leering at him. A light turned on from inside the house and Cole looked up to see the old man's face. Dressed like a ringleader from a travelling circus in the 1930's, he had a long, black beard and wore a top hat.

"Help me!" Cole cried out, sobbing.

The old man smiled, snapped his fingers, and closed the blinds. Cole ran towards the front yard, but his Vans melted away with each step. He felt a chill radiating throughout his body and looked down to find that the skin of his feet had begun to change color. His stomach churned and he felt a need to vomit, but nothing came out but cold air. His tears instantly froze into shards of ice which he could feel tearing through the ducts of his eyes. He tried to scream as his senses failed, but he had no last words.

He had no last thoughts.

THE NEXT MORNING, Jerry Anderson, President of the Greenfields HOA, woke to a startling notification on NextDoor:

My son Cole is missing!
Please let me know if you've seen him.

BAD PRESS WAS about the worst thing he could imagine for his line of work, so he got dressed and figured he'd head to meet with Mr. and Mrs. Messner to get the scoop before the media or police caught wind of a potentially missing kid. He hopped in his Mercedes Maybach and took a right onto Locust Avenue. Something unusual caught his eyes and he slammed on the brakes, skidding to a stop in front of the old man's house.

"Oh my God," he said.

"That is the most beautiful winter display I have ever seen." He snapped a selfie, smiling with the dozens of snowmen behind him and posted it to the Greenfields HOA Facebook page.

"I really need to do something about that door-knob," he said.

IT'S NOT ALWAYS WHY

Her footsteps pattered along cream colored ceramic tiles. She marveled at their smooth texture, a feeling that she had never experienced prior to the clock striking midnight as she entered the glass sliding doors of the emergency room.

It was her 13th birthday.

The bottoms of her feet were rough with callouses, no stranger to the unforgiving terrain of the Shenandoah Mountains. She smiled. The sensation felt good. However, it was crucial that her focus remained on the task at hand. A task that had her mind centered around a question that all teenagers struggle with, the question of purpose.

Why?

I want to know why.

The family prepared her for this moment for as long as she could remember. She studied maps, learned how to fend off attacks from behind, and hiked ten miles a day through the woodlands, in order to build up stamina for the ceremony later. Her bare shoulders were lined with scars from a short, but fruitful lifetime of punishment. She was allowed to pick the switch for Him, but the Father's strikes were swift and merciless if she deviated from tradition, questioned His authority, or found herself in a situation deemed morally compromising.

Her eternal questions remained internal.

She walked through the sterile hallways of a small hospital in Verbena, Virgina, a ghost in a white dress given to her by her birth mother. The other mothers had presents waiting in the hollow too, tokens that would only come after a rite that was older than anything that the girl could comprehend. She could not read, but she knew the symbols and floor plan necessary to locate the maternity ward.

A doctor in operating scrubs rushed past her, his head swimming in stress. It was remarkable how far she traveled into the hospital before seeing another person. She gazed at his clothing in sheer awe and found herself reaching out to grab the teal material, a color she had never seen before. The surgeon's aide disappeared around a sharp corner, leaving her alone in the unnatural silence. She continued moving down the hallway, when a deep voice called out behind her.

"Excuse me, Miss. Are you lost?"

She turned around and locked eyes with the shape

of a uniformed man the Father had warned her about. A well meaning night watchman approached her with kind eyes and leaned down on one knee in order to be level with the petite barefoot girl in the white dress.

"I can help you find your parents if you tell me where they might be, darlin," he said.

She said nothing in response.

"That sure is a pretty dress you have on. Can I at least have your name?"

The girl reached into a small pocket on the left side of her dress and removed a small, sharp blade. The man caught a glimpse of light reflecting off of the edge in the moment before she ran it across, and into, the jugular vein of his neck.

Her practice with livestock paid off.

The cut was deep and effective. The guard fell backwards onto the tile floor as the wound sprayed steady pumps of blood high onto the wall behind him. He attempted to call for help on his radio, but the shock and trauma to his neck left him unable to do anything but try and stop the bleeding. His attempts failed. His eyes bulged with fear while he bled out, the soles of his rubber boots squeaking, kicking the tile floor to the dying beats of his heart. The girl continued moving down the hallway, undisturbed. Her feet left tiny, bloody footprints along the way. A trail to a fresh corpse.

She arrived at the maternity ward to find a half dozen newborns asleep in the nursery.

I want to know why.

She watched as two nurses checked vitals and scribbled notes across wooden clipboards. The infants shocked the girl with their quiet demeanors. She had participated in a few birthing ceremonies and the little things always screamed themselves into consciousness. She peered behind a pane of glass at the miscellaneous rows of babies.

"Do not worry, for you shall know which one is His," the Father had told her before she departed from the hollow.

Under the dim fluorescent lights, she waited for one of the nurses to exit the room. It was time to put the Father's training to use. She crept inside and moved down an aisle as the lone nurse washed her hands at a small sink. The girl ambushed the nurse with a calculated series of strikes that packed the punch, ferocity, and aggression of a trained assassin. Her first stab punctured a kidney. Before the nurse had the chance to react, the girl leapt onto her back, put her arms around her throat, and pulled her backwards onto the floor. Her second strike tore into the trachea. The nurse attempted to scream, but the only sound that escaped was a disgusting burst of air that gurgled through the newly exposed anatomy of the nurse's throat. The third and final strike landed at the perfect angle to piece her heart. For the nurse, it felt like forever, but the moment was quick, efficient, and there was little commotion. The babies continued to sleep in the afterglow of their laborious delivery.

The girl rose from the floor to find a beam of fluorescent light illuminating the facial features of an infant in the center of the room.

Alone in the light, she took this as her sign.

The child wore a tiny blue cap and was swaddled in a cotton blanket. The girl picked up the child and cradled him against her bloodstained chest as if she was his mother.

"Shhhhh," she said, rocking the sleeping boy in her arms. "You'll be safe with me, little one. We're leaving now."

She took the small bed sheet and wrapped the child around her chest with an improvised carrier. She left the room, hit the nearest stairwell, and walked down three flights of stairs before exiting through an emergency door on the ground level. Their exit triggered an alarm and caused the child to cry out in the dead of the Virginia night. The girl sang to him.

"Look up, my child," she said.

The warm, humid, and cloudless sky was filled with stars. The girl wasted no time admiring the brilliant view, running towards the nearby woods adjacent to the parking lot. She weaved through a few rows of empty cars, trucks, and SUVs and disappeared into the tree line as a whirl of sirens, emergency vehicles arriving to the hospital, filled the air.

The next phase of the rite began.

I want to know why.

For two miles, she ran. She did not stop. She did not think. She just ran. She arrived at the shallow bank of the South Fork River and hopped across a series of large rocks with the muscle memory of an olympic athlete. When she reached the other side of the bank, she stopped at a large maple tree that was marked with a red circle. She retrieved a small woven bag that hung from one of its lower branches and pulled out a few strips of jerky, a small bottle, and a single serving of infant formula. They needed to eat. The girl sat at the base of the maple while the infant took the nipple of the bottle, instinctively consuming the ounce of liquid.

"Everything here," the girl said, pointing at the environment around them, "was made by Him. The trees, the water, the rocks. We are the dust that fell from the stars to become the clay from which He molded us."

When the child finished, she placed him across her scarred shoulder, tapping his back to help him digest his first meal in the real world.

"We are nothing, and He is everything."

She spoke like a well trained parrot.

The Father would be proud.

They continued moving through the dense forest. Her pace slowed, but her steps kept their urgency. The eight mile route had been timed, rehearsed, and choreographed for months. Some trips she had made with the family, but she had grown acclimated to making the five hour trek alone. An hour had passed when they started to pick up elevation. Along the hike, the girl knew where to find clean water, where to turn, and where to avoid loose rocks. Her eyes had adapted to the darkness like a nocturnal animal and the density of the woodlands did nothing to deter the girl in the bloody dress. If the child cried, she sang to him and rocked the pouch back and forth until he fell back asleep.

The red circles began to appear on the tree trunks with greater frequency.

They neared the hollow.

The pair descended a steep slope when the girl caught the flickering light from a torch about a half mile to the north. As they moved closer to the flame, additional torches began to appear.

I want to know why.

The path transitioned into a comfortable walking trail underneath her feet. She was thankful. As she approached the first torch she could see that all of the members of the family had positioned themselves along the trail in two rows that faced each other. They were adorned in red hooded robes. As she passed each family member, they kneeled to the ground in silence. She began passing the wooden cabins of their homes, when a large bonfire came into her view. Its flames towered high into the air at the center of their settlement. Adjacent to the flames, the Father stood at the top of a large, wooden platform, holding his hands above his head. Unlike the rest of the family, his robe was white. The girl held the child a little bit tighter as she moved towards the fire. The red robed mothers slowly circled them, still holding their torches.

"You have succeeded and brought fortune upon our lives, my child," he said.

"I did everything as asked, as instructed, and as rehearsed," the girl replied in a careful tone of respect. She removed the boy from the carrier and lifted him towards the Father, making sure he could get a good look at the infant.

"Leave the child in the basket," the Father said.

At the bottom of the platform lay a small wicker basket lined with white cotton pillows and covered in a layer of geranium petals. The girl was nervous, but she did not dare express it in any discernible manner. She knelt in front of the Father and placed the newborn onto the flowers. It began to cry and the girl could feel tears welling in the corners of her face. She did her best to stifle the urge. The basket was connected to a rope and pulley that the Father began to bring upwards. The mothers sang a solemn hymn.

"Tonight, our family gains a mother and loses a son, for His will is the way, and the way is His will," the Father said, holding the basket above his head.

"His will is the way," the mothers replied.

The girl put her hands above her head. She couldn't help herself.

She cried.

"Voluntatis est via eius," the Father said, slicing into the palm of his hand with a knife. He let a droplet of blood fall onto the forehead of the child and there was a sudden eruption of what sounded like thunder to the girl.

A massive hand, attached to something so large it could not be seen from the hollow, peeled back the tree line, reached down to grab the basket with its God-like fingers, and pulled the child up into the infinite sky.

The girl looked up, realizing that the important question is not always, why.

I want to know how.

I want to know how.

I want to know how.

I want to know who.

I want to know who.

I want to know who.

THE STRANGER IN THE SQUARED
CIRCLE

I was 29 years old when I saw a dead body for the first time. Up to that point, I had watched my fair share of true crime documentaries and I once administered CPR to an elderly man at an ice skating rink death-seizing in cardiac arrest, but I had an otherwise plain life and relatively few morbid encounters before that day. I'm lucky, I guess.

Some people probably think they have a good idea of how they'd react in that situation, but I honestly hadn't given it much thought until I locked eyes with the shriveled husk of a man in the alley behind Gino's Gym. It was Wednesday.

Leg day.

Gino had given me a key to the back door of his gym and allowed me to come in and use his equipment in the hours before it opened because I was a local amateur wrestling hero. I went 178-0 in high school and won the state title three times. My name carries more weight around Lorain County than what I can currently deadlift and trust me, that's a lot of weight.

That morning I was so focused on pushing my PR's for barbell back squats, goblet rear-foot-elevated split squats, and explosive lunges, that I didn't even notice the body on my way in. I walked right past it, pruned skin and all. One might wonder how this happened, but the corpse was so disfigured I could barely tell what it was. It had been propped up against a dumpster lining the brick exterior wall of the gym and its arms and legs were, for all intents and purposes, skeletal. It had no noticeable muscles, organs, or any sort of blood visible. It looked like the yellow, hollow shell that cicadas leave on the branches of trees after they moult. The only way I could even understand what it was, was by recognizing the terrified expression of receding eyes in a skull that was clinging on for dear life to its spinal column.

It was Gino.

Okay, so here's how I reacted to a dead body:

I threw up in the alley. Don't judge me.

I WAS on my way out of the detective's office when Jim Morris called me. It had been a while since I heard the shrill drawl of Virginia's most lovable carny.

"Luke? How the hell are ya?" he asked.

I got behind the wheel of my beat up F-150 and began to head back to the fleabag where I spent my weeknights.

"I've been better. I just spent the morning talking with the police. Some sick son of a bitch bled Gino completely dry," I said.

"Jesus Christ. Say your Hail Marys. That doesn't sound like any sort of business I'd ever want to catch myself tangled up in."

He paused.

"How's the weather up there? It's hotter than a jalapeños coochie down here right now."

Jim would only call me to cash in a favor and I owed him more than a few. I remained silent, waiting for him to cut to the chase. As the head promoter and owner of SVW, Shenandoah Valley Wrestling, I knew it wouldn't take him long.

"Ok, I won't give you the runaround, Luke. I'm in kind of a pickle here," he said.

More silence.

"I've been running all over Hell's half acre trying to get all my ducks in a row for the biggest show I've ever booked and Silverback just went AWOL after his most recent match in Mexico and he was at the top of the card. I heard that big fucker tried to hang with El Diablo Rojo in a lucha match."

I couldn't help but laugh picturing Glenn "Silver-back" Davis wrestling lucha style. At 375 pounds, he could barely make it to the ring before blowing up. In the few matches I had with him, I quickly learned to play it slow and brace for stiff chops. That was the only trick in his limited move set, but even the most hardcore wrestling crowds loved him. He was a throwback, a sideshow attraction from the bygone eras of territorial wrestling. I found my curiosity pointing towards Jim's "biggest show ever." He is a wrestling promoter. Every show is the biggest show ever.

"What's the line up?" I asked him. I could hear him get excited through the phone.

"Alright, buckle up. This weekend I've got the Backyard Boys in a ladder match with T.R.U., Keith Rodgers and The Freak in a hardcore ladder match, Shirley Temple and Vicky Knox, and a triple threat between Al Laymon, Vince Barker, and Monty Ketchum. Glenn was set to take on The Stranger to close out the show and send the folks home happy. If I can't give them Silverback, a surprise appearance by the golden boy, Luke R. Cade, will do just fine, you superstar you."

I had to hand it to him. For SVW, this was a hell of a card. It would definitely pack the Greene County VFW where Jim put on his small, but nationally respected events. Calling me a superstar was a rib. He must have heard about Japan.

"You heard about JPWL?" I asked.

"It was only a matter of time, pal," he said. I could

hear his gap toothed and genuine grin through the phone.

Two weeks ago I got the call to join the JPWL's Summer Showdown, one of the premiere indie wrestling events in the world. My weekends on the road hitting gyms and bingo halls for gas money had come to an end for now. I'd be nowhere without Jim, the old school promoter who let me sublet his basement apartment for free while I spent my weekends training. I had a little over a month to go before my flights out to Japan, so I didn't have an excuse to say anything but yes. Not that I could ever say no to Jim Morris, Virginia's most lovable carny.

"Anything you need, Jim. I'll see you this weekend."

"That's my boy, Luke. That's my boy," he said. And with that, he hung up.

I pulled into the parking lot of my apartment complex and realized that unlike everyone else on the card, I had absolutely know idea who "The Stranger" was.

"CLIMB on outta that truck and let me take a good look at you," Jim said. He had aged tremendously since I saw him last. I hated thinking it, but he looked like shit.

"Don't say what you're thinking Luke, I know I

look like ten miles of bad road," he said, extending his arms for a bear hug. I obliged. It was good to see the only father figure I had in life, even if he looked like a cry for help.

"Brenda left me last fall. Finally got fed up with all of my bullshit," he said.

"I'm sorry to hear that."

I unloaded my duffel bag from the back of my truck and caught a Miller Lite Jim tossed at me, testing my reflexes.

"She put up with me longer than most would have, that's for sure," he said, laughing as we cracked open our beers. We knocked them back before I even had a chance to get my stuff inside his house.

Jim grilled up a couple of T-Bone steaks while the sun set over the Blue Ridge Mountains, burning the horizon. We shot the shit about the business which, according to Jim, was good. I brought him up to speed about my run through the U.K. and ongoing feud with The Sanitarium. Jim found it hilarious that Will E. Finster wrestled in a straight jacket.

"You're telling me that little fucker never takes it off during the match?" he asked, slurping down the mashed insides of a baked potato like it was an oyster.

"Never. Not once. His move set is mostly kip ups and kicks, but he pops the crowd with suicide dives and all sorts of athletic moves you have to see to believe and it works, somehow," I said, chewing a piece of steak. I skipped the potato. I don't eat carbs after six p.m.

"I don't understand your generation at all. For the first time in my life, I wake up and feel completely out of touch," he said.

We sat on his patio and talked ring psychology for what felt like hours. I picked his brain about high spots and hot tags and saw his eyes light up like the ass ends of the fireflies which danced in his backyard. When I was around Jim, I was a sponge. He wasn't nearly as out of touch as he thought himself to be. Wrestling is a hard business to make money in and while Jim wasn't wealthy, he had shelter, food, and respect in the indus-try. I admired him for it. Then, I asked him a question that had been running through my mind since I agreed to help.

"Tell me about The Stranger," I said.

Jim's expression shifted slightly. I couldn't exactly tell what was going through his mind, but his back stiff-ened and he crossed his arms. After a moment of hesi-tation, he poured two fingers of bourbon into a stainless steel tumbler and offered me the bottle. I declined, waiting for his response.

"I'll be honest with you Luke, I don't know a whole lot about him. It's the damnedest thing. I know a few folks have been trying to get him booked stateside for years but they could never make it happen. Walt Trubiski almost got him to MMW a couple years ago and Cooper Bennett swears he wrestled for WPWL but I don't believe anything that fucker says. He's only got one oar in the water, if you know what I mean," he said. He polished off the whiskey in one long gulp.

"So you're telling me I have to get in the ring tomorrow with talent you don't know anything about? Can you vouch for him? Is he safe?" I asked. My mind raced with all sorts of questions.

"Well, I can't vouch for him personally obviously, but I've seen him on tape and he's solid. He's a general. You'd have the night off," he said.

"What do you mean, you've seen him on tape?" I asked. I was annoyed and confused, but curious. I grew up trading tapes and studied all of the underground legends: Brutus Hancock, Heath Lunderstrom, Mauga. I had no recollection in my time as a fan or my time on the circuit ever hearing about The Stranger. It was odd.

"What is his gimmick?" I asked.

Jim poured himself another round.

"You wouldn't believe me if I told you. Let's go inside and I'll show you the tape."

———

THE FOOTAGE IS black and white and appears to be waterlogged. A massive crowd, easily in the thousands, sits submissively. Each member wears a white button down shirt and light khakis and they collectively keep their hands folded across their laps. They stare, zombie like, as two men enter a ring that is simple, yet elegant.   There is no referee, no ring announcer, and no way to tell exactly where the match is taking place.   The two men move to opposite ring corners, squatting in yoga-like poses.   There is no audio and it looks like it was originally shot on 8mm film.   It's jittery and chaotic.

One man is built like a brick house, a barrel chested mammoth who is clearly pushing seven feet in height and 400 pounds in weight.   He wears black trunks and his sledgehammer sized fists are covered in talc.   He is bald and sports an outrageously large handlebar mustache.

The other man is lean, but muscular.   He is of average height and has long black hair which he wears down across his shoulders.   He wears black pants and a black jacket of some kind.   He is not nearly as physically intimidating as the larger gentleman, but there is something odd in his ring presence that I find enthralling.   I look over at Jim, who is smiling at the sheer strangeness of everything that is taking place on the screen.

The two wrestlers stand, face each other, and bow. I don't hear a bell, but it is apparent that the match has begun.   The big man immediately hits the ropes and attempts a clothesline but the dark haired man dodges it with the grace of a ballet dancer.   He spins underneath the forward thrusting bicep and counters with a kick to the big man's back knee that sends him buckling to the ground. It is a stiff shot. The big man grimaces in pain but quickly manages to grab the lean man by the throat with his meat hooks. The crowd continues staring into space, not reacting in any way to the physical match taking place in the ring.

"Is this strong style?"

Jim doesn't answer.

I continue to watch as the big man rains his fists down onto the lean man's face. His closed fists connect against flesh in three successive strikes. The third hit opens a gash under the lean man's right eye that begins gushing blood on to the mat. Opened up the hard way, I grow nervous that this is some sort of deathmatch. Honestly, I'm not quite sure what I'm watching. It's seemingly more akin to M.M.A. then Pro Wrestling. As blood continues to hit the mat, I notice the lean man is smiling. No, he is laughing.

The big man brings up his right leg and brings it down with enough force to cave in the lean man's skull but he rolls out of the way and kips up with the smoothest form I've ever seen.

"Holy shit."

"Shh. Keep watching," Jim says.

The lean man leaps to the top of the ring post nearest to the big man in one swift move and turns 180 degrees so that he is facing him. He perches on the post like a gargoyle and then hits the big man with the most brutal missile dropkick I've ever seen. Dazed, the big man throws a series of punches that the lean man dodges like Ali roping a dope. The big man grows frustrated and climbs under the ropes and reaches under the ring. He retrieves something small and sharp looking and taunts the lean man.

"Is that a knife?"

"Shh! *Keep watching*," he says again.

The big man charges with what becomes clear is a five inch blade of some kind. He stabs at the lean man's chest, but his movements are reckless. The lean man side steps a forward thrust and positions his hands on the large wrist of the big man.

What happens next, happens in a flash.

The lean man twists the wrist and propels it into the upper chest cavity of the big man, who drops to his knees. The blade is buried deep. The lean man then runs to the top rope and does a lionsault that ends with his legs driving the big man's head directly into the mat, face first. The big man loses consciousness. The lean man rolls the big man onto his back and then straddles his waist. The vast crowd stands in unison, expressionless. The lean man bites into the neck of the big man and the tape ends, ending the silence with a piercing blast of static black and white snow.

"What the hell did I just watch, Jim?"

He bursts out into gleeful laughter.

"The Stranger has a Vampire gimmick, the best one I've ever seen!" he cackles so hard he loses his breath and it takes him a second to gain his composure. I am not amused.

"That dumb bastard has worked himself into a shoot!"

Now I had a truly good reason to be nervous.

IT FRUSTRATED me that Jim didn't think there was anything off putting about the tape he had just played for me in the VCR of his den.

"Thanks for showing me a snuff film, asshole," I said.

"Oh for heaven's sake, that was a gimmicked knife and some basic stage theatrics. Those fuckers in eastern Europe may put on shows a little differently than how we do it here, but mark my words, both of us are gonna be legends in this business for finally getting The Stranger into an American ring."

"You're already a legend."

I knew Jim would never be satisfied with his life, no matter how much success came his way. He was a promoter and when this show was over and the lights in the venue had been shut off, he would already be busy planning his next show, his next attraction. He would probably die alone feeling no true sense of accomplishment. He was chasing something that was as imaginary as the results of our choreographed bouts of good vs. evil.

"This is all I have," he said. The desperation in his voice caught me off guard. "You saw how he moved in that ring. You two are going to go out there and put on a clinic. A five star match."

"Don't flatter me, Jim."

"Just get some rest, my boy. You're calling the match and The Stranger is taking the pin. You'll have 45 minutes to prove why JPWL called you up."

"Are we at the VFW?"

Jim burst into a hearty laugh.

"No, my boy. Once I got The Stranger booked the dirt sheets brought the card enough interest to get the show moved to the Blue Ridge Hall. It sold out in 15 minutes," he said. The Blue Ridge Hall, with standing room, can seat 1000 indie wrestling fans, a far cry from the usual 300 or so hardcore fans that typically packed the VFW for his cards.

He wasn't kidding.

This was his biggest show ever.

———

THE NEXT AFTERNOON, I pulled up to the Blue Ridge Hall with only one thing on my mind: I needed to find The Stranger, size him up, and talk over a few spot ideas before our match. One of my strengths in the ring is improvisation, but all I knew about the guy was that he was fast, flew high, and likely killed a man in some sort of bizarre ritual deathmatch. I just wanted to send the crowd home happy as a thank you to Jim before I took off for Japan.

Upon getting out of my truck I caught Vicky Knox warming up with some high knees in the parking lot. She had shaved the side of her head, dyed her hair black, and gauged her ears since the last time I saw her. Despite being five feet tall, Vicky looked like she could scrap with anyone.

"Look at you, Mr. JPWL," she said. I gave her a hug and laughed off her sarcastic tone. I was going to hear it all night long.

"Yeah, yeah. Have you seen Jim?" I asked.

"I think he's inside making sure the bar has enough booze for the marks tonight. I'm about to go run the ropes for a few minutes if you want to come," she said.

I took a second to think about it because cardio sure sounded like a good idea. I needed anything to ease my tension a bit, but thanks to my obsession, I decided to pick her brain instead.

"You know anything about The Stranger?" I asked.

"Not really, but it's the only damn thing I've heard anyone here talk about this morning, so I'm looking forward to catching your match. No one has gotten a look at him since he arrived."

"Wait, he's here?"

She finished taping up her wrists, grabbed a duffel bag from her trunk, and slammed the lid of her Civic shut. As the hatch closed, a large, silver Airstream trailer came into my view. It sat on the other side of the gravel parking lot underneath the shade of a large elm tree.

"As far as everyone knows, he's in there."

"Thanks Vicky," I said, walking towards the trailer. "Oh, what do you think for the end spot tonight? 450 splash off the balcony, or double counter into the Arcade Machine?"

She laughed. "They're going to be so damn wasted that they'll cheer for anything in order to put themselves over. Don't be a jackass. Work smart and save your one good knee for Japan."

It was good advice. I raised my hand in acknowledgement and continued walking towards the trailer, which I could now see was connected to a flawless, black Chevy Silverado with heavily tinted windows. I admired the truck for a second before knocking on the door of the trailer, which also had the brand new smell. Its chrome exterior gleamed with fresh polish and radiated heat from the Virginia sun. Goddamn, it was humid. No one answered, so I knocked again.

I felt myself growing impatient. Here I was, a true student of the industry, and it bothered me to no end that I had never heard of The Stranger. To make matters worse, I couldn't get Jim's tape to stop playing on a loop in my head. Seeing that knife plunge into a human chest so easily, I wondered how it could have been gimmicked. I've seen guys take weed eaters to their backs, fall into tubes of fluorescent lights, bump into tables covered in razor wire.

We sacrifice our bodies and spill our blood to enter-
tain, amuse, and shock, but that video was different.
I wanted to truly understand what I was dealing
with, so I turned the handle of the trailer and heard
it click open with ease. It was unlocked. I pulled
open the door and was immediately hit with a
strange odor. It reminded me of my grandmother's
closet.

Moth balls, maybe?

"Hey, it's Luke. I was wondering if I could come in
and talk over some spots for the show tonight," I said.

No one answered.

It was so damn dark in the windowless trailer that I
could hardly see the interior, but I was going to figure
out this mess one way or another, so I stepped inside
and the door closed behind me. In the total darkness, I
could hear some sort of A/C unit running. The trailer
was frigid, a welcome contrast from the cruel summer
that had been beating down on me just moments
before. I pulled up my phone and cranked the bright-
ness up so I could orient myself in the pitch black
room.

The trailer was sleek, modern, and clearly cost
more than what any wrestler I knew could afford. It
made me wonder why he booked with Jim, who was
likely paying him a couple hundred, tops. I walked
down a kitchen area that was set up with gorgeous
stainless steel appliances and black marble counter-
tops. On the opposite side of the trailer, I could see a

black leather sofa. I heard nothing but the fan blowing.

"Hello?" I said, again, to no response.

Eventually, I got to a small bedroom that was outfitted with a queen size mattress and my eye caught something odd at the foot of the bed: a large, wooden chest that was tightly latched at six different points. It looked fairly old, which made it stand out compared to the modern luxury design of the rest of the trailer. I figured it was full of ring gear. I was about to leave and head into the hall in order to find Jim, when I got an inkling to open the box. I guess I was just curious and figured The Stranger owed it to me. I needed some sort of answer from this visit, so I popped open the latches, took a deep breath, and opened the box.

I shuddered upon seeing what was inside.

It wasn't ring gear.

The light from my phone exposed the features of a human who was in an impossible shape, pretzeled inside like an acrobat at the circus, but unwilling. I could tell that they were once muscular and enormous, but somehow their body had atrophied into a horrific set of angles that turned my stomach. Then, the head turned towards me and moaned.

"Oh fuck," I said, stumbling, falling onto my ass.

"Pllleassssee. Hellllllpp meeeeeee," they whispered through a set of lips that screamed for water. As they shifted towards me, I noticed that they were wearing a wrestling unitard with a silver stripe down the middle, embroidered with the letters S-B.

The frail man in the box was Glenn "Silverback" Davis, the monster of the indie circuit. The monster that went missing in Mexico. I began to dial 911 when a shadow moved out of the corner of my eye and in a flash, I lost consciousness.

I WOKE on the floor of the trailer in a state of pure delirium. My head was pounding, the result of being struck by some sort of blunt object. As I came to my senses, I pictured the nightmare inside The Stranger's box. I needed to gather my bearings and find Jim. Thanks to a bedside LED nightlight I could see inside the bedroom now. The chest, my cell phone, and whoever assaulted me were missing. I stumbled out of the trailer and it became clear that a few hours had passed. The parking lot was full of cars and the sun had fallen. Even from outside, I could hear the unmistakable roar of a crowd and the sounds of bodies hitting the stretched canvas mat. I made it to the front door of the Blue Ridge Hall, where I found Monty Ketchum smoking a cigarette.

"Holy shit dude, Jim has been going berserk in there thinking you flaked," he said.

"I...need...to...find...Jim," I said.

"Bro, come on. Let's get to the side entrance. You're up next."

All of this felt wrong. Surreal. I felt like I was hovering outside of my body watching the madness take place overhead. I was so shaken I couldn't seem to explain to Monty what was going on. He led me to a door which opened to the event staging area. I caught the eyes of The Backyard Boys and they looked at me like I was crazy. Maybe I was.

"Go get em, Luke," Monty said, pushing me towards the red curtain that led to the ring. I took a deep breath and began to bring up the box when my entrance music hit. I parted the curtain and the dozens of bright stage lights blinded me. I was hit with the smell of stale light beer and body odor. As the 8-bit chiptune played, the crowd went apeshit upon the anticipation of my arrival, screaming with a frenzy that I'm not sure I had experienced in my time in the squared circle.

"Yes, Yes, Yes," they chanted.

I scanned the area for Jim while I performed my carefully rehearsed movements to the ring and did my best to soldier on without making my hesitations and knowledge of the ominous obvious.

"You good, Luke?" Marty, the veteran SVW referee, asked me.

"I need a hot mic," I said.

The crowd continued singing along with my theme in a hedonistic trance. The energy in the room was palpable. Marty handed me a mic. I rolled under the first rope and stood up in the ring.

"Everyone, listen," I said as the music continued pumping through a large PA system. The crowd continued singing along, ignoring my request. I lost my patience.

"I said listen to me you fucking morons. This is important."

In an instant, the crowd started booing, assuming that I had decided to play the heel tonight.

"Our admission pays your rent, we don't have to listen to a spot monkey," a large fan in a Mauga shirt screamed at me while drinking from a tall can of PBR. His buddies slapped him across the shoulders, laughing in delight.

"Someone is going to die tonight," I said, pleading with them. This only incensed the crowd further. Someone in the back row started chanting "Stranger, Stranger, Stranger..." and it quickly spread throughout the large hall, a virus of stupidity. I continued to look for Jim, but I couldn't make him out in the sea of fans who jeered at me.

The lights went out.

The crowd gasped in surprise at the sudden shift into total darkness. A few fans woo'd. Some laughed, trying to cut the tension in the room. I felt my skin break out into a sweat as the seconds passed, when I heard a faint noise growing in the center of the ring. It wasn't a recognizable pitch, it was some kind of sonic vibration which started in my ears and radiated throughout the marrow of my bones. It was an eerie sensation, like being stuck in the middle of a set of train tracks as an engine sped towards me. The vibration grew louder. Then, a lone spotlight hit the ceiling of Blue Ridge Hall, where The Stranger appeared hovering in the middle of the air.

"HO-LY SHIT, HO-LY SHIT, HO-LY SHIT," the crowd said.

I stood there dumbfounded in the ring as The Stranger slowly descended in the air. There were no wires or zip lines connected to his body, which was donned in a thick black robe.

The bastard was floating.

I backed up into a turnbuckle, watching this David Blaine styled illusion take place to the soundtrack of the bizarre vibration which continued to shake my skull. The descent lasted fifteen seconds altogether and ended as the stage lights came back on. At last, I was face to face with The Stranger.

The crowd continued to pop as I locked eyes with the undeniable force in front of me. He lifted his arms and the robe fell to the mat. He looked exactly the same as the figure I saw wrestle on Jim's tape. He was tall, pale, and lean. However, this close I could see that his body was covered in scars. Hundreds of them. His eyes were silver. Pure silver. I was unsure of how to proceed, when he broke the silence in a voice that sent shivers down my spine.

"I came here for you, Luke," he said. I felt a lump in my throat. I was unable to swallow. Unable to respond. I didn't need to. He kept talking. "Every second of your life. Every road you've traveled. Every single mile has led you to this moment right now. This moment here with me. Here with them." He gestured towards the crowd, who screamed his name.

"Let's go STRAN-GER," they said.

I finally worked up the courage to respond.

"Why did you hurt Glenn?" I asked.

"Because I wasn't going to waste this opportunity in the ring with someone who pretends to be a gorilla," he said, his lips curling into a smile. "And, I was hungry."

"I'm sure you've hurt plenty of people before," I said.

"Humans like to suspend their disbelief, which works wonders for folks like me." He opened his mouth slightly to reveal a set of fangs that would have looked comical if I hadn't seen the results of how he put them to use.

"What do you want from me," I said.

"I want the same exact thing you want, Luke. The same thing you're chasing. Let's give them a show."

He leapt to the top turnbuckle and backflipped onto the mat in one motion before bowing his head. The crowd ate it up as I took off my shirt and stretched my arms. He was right. Somehow, I understood that everything had led to this moment. Every match in high school. My ACL tear. The hard work in the gym. The hours I spent studying the greats.

I wasn't going to back down.

I gave The Stranger two middle fingers and the crowd roared in excitement.

"Ok, you've got it."

Marty rang the bell.

I've wrestled 647 matches across the world with hundreds of wrestlers. Ring chemistry is as real and as measurable as romantic chemistry.

You either have it, or you don't.

When we locked up for our first move exchange, I felt connected to The Stranger in a way that I had never experienced in any of my previous showdowns in the squared circle. I didn't need to call my moves. I didn't need to think about what was next in our chain of combinations. Wrestling The Stranger was easier than breathing and we spoke the same language. For the first few minutes of the match, we teased the crowd with a series of lock ups, counters, and near take-downs. I went for an arm drag that he somehow countered into a German suplex that sent me flying across the ring. I was stunned. He was so goddamn strong. He worked stiff, but I could tell he was holding back. We worked up to a spot where we went back and forth with a few chops and the crowd groaned as we traded blows. We traded high spots and finisher kick outs that teased the crowd into a frenzy. We went 20 minutes, then 45, then 60.

It was the best match I've ever wrestled and the euphoric response from the crowd proved it.

The Stranger got me in a rear choke submission hold that could have ended it all, when I caught Jim in the crowd. He was smiling, ear to ear. A proud father and even prouder promoter.

This truly was his biggest show ever.

I noticed he had a large piece of gauze taped around his neck, when The Stranger whispered into my ear.

"We are destined to do this forever," he said.

I felt him bite deeply into my neck and watched as a thick spray of arterial blood hit the fans in the front row. He let go of me and I fell to the mat, bleeding hard on the canvas. I put my hand up to the wound to stop it from spilling, but it was useless. The two large punctures had sprayed into The Strangers face, covering his jaws. I lay on my back as the crowd reached the apex of their united celebration. A pop that would be immortalized in the history of indie wrestling.

"THIS-IS-AWE-SOME," they said, clapping.

The Stranger stood in the center of the ring with his black boot on my chest and a thick, crimson mask dripping down his chin.

Marty made the count.

"1."

I should have been dying from blood loss, but I felt an energy pulsing through my veins at a furious pace.

In some space of my consciousness, it became clear that Luke was dead and gone.

"2."

Wrestling is the only thing I know and the only thing I love.

"3."

I'm a stranger now too, I guess.

TOASTED

In a dimly lit living room, Rachel paced.

"I am done," she said.

A thick layer of tin foil and painter's tape covered the large front window, preventing her from knowing the time of day. The less Rachel knew about the world outside, the better.

The stench of unwashed body parts thickened the air around her. Empty boxes littered the floor, stacked, Jenga-like, in corners and on side tables, leaving her couch hidden. Like a crazed ballerina, she gracefully danced in between the dozens of cardboard carcasses which once held kitchen appliances: bread makers, mixers, blenders, and microwaves. The thousands of white packing peanuts scattered across the floor created an illusion that it had snowed an inch inside of the home. Each step she took crunched, creating an abrasive squeal of bare skin sliding along styrofoam.

"We both know that this is a lie," a toaster from inside her kitchen eventually replied. Sweaty, tired, and nervous, Rachel whimpered.

"You promised that this would end," she said.

"And we are *so* close," the toaster cooed, as if Rachel was an overtired infant in need of breast milk.

"No, I am done," Rachel said, looking out the peephole of her front door. A vinyl record spun on a turntable somewhere nearby, but its song had finished long ago. Now, it just popped and crackled in an endless, hypnotizing loop.

An hour passed, but Rachel's right eye remained fixed to the peephole. A Greenfields mail truck slowly pulled into view and she watched as the driver got out and carried a small white box over to the cement stoop of her unremarkable ranch style house. The driver didn't linger, somehow keenly aware that something was wrong inside the walls of 1210 Poplar Street.

Rachel opened the door just long enough to move the package behind the front door. Using a box cutter, she meticulously cut through the packing tape as if she were performing open heart surgery. Unlike the previous cache of boxes she had opened in this living room, this one contained 100 rounds of 5.56 caliber, NATO grade ammunition. Rachel began to bash her head into the thick cedar door.

"This is over…"

Bash.

"This is over…"

Bash.

On the third concussion, her forehead split open, leaving a thick smear of blood on the white paint of the door.

"Get on with it," the toaster commanded.

Rachel grabbed an AR-15 rifle which was propped up near the living room couch, loaded its magazine, and chambered a round. Then, she put the barrel under her chin and pulled the trigger.

A week passed before a neighbor jogging by called security due to the smell emanating from inside the house. Local police officers discovered Rachel's body, along with the strange stockpile of appliances. They also found the decapitated body of her husband sitting serenely at their breakfast table.

A stainless steel toaster had been duct taped to his neck.

TEDDY

Time is a funny thing. I wake up some days thinking today is the day I'm gonna get shot down in a plane, but then I try to get out of bed and remember that I'm just old, wrinkled, and alone. I don't know where that time went, but I've seen enough to know that this world ain't ever gonna change.

I DIDN'T SELL my soul to the Devil like Robert Johnson did, but trust me, I could have many times. Everyone wonders what His face looks like, but the truth of the matter is that the Devil ain't got no face. He is real though, sure as shit makes shrooms.

I found the Devil in 43' while I was navigating with the 99th Pursuit Squadron stationed in North Africa. At some point I became good friends with a medic from Georgia named Beau, who passed me a plain looking silver ring one evening before he got deployed to Sicily to go help clean up the mess.

"Get rid of this, quietly," he said to me.

I don't know why he gave that ring to me, and to this day I have no idea where it came from. All I know is that ring had the Devil in it. I woke up every night that it sat in my pocket with visions of horrible things in my head that made the days watching my friends get shot down in overmatched P-40s seem like R&R. I heard voices. I didn't eat and barely drank anything for two solid weeks. Some nights, I swear something would sit on my back and suck the soul out of my body while I was asleep, but I couldn't tell you how it worked or what it looked like.

Beau never told me where to go or what to do with the ring, but I figured I wasn't supposed to just drop it off in a thunder beam, so I waited until we were escorting some friendlies to Libya and at the first opportunity I had, I tossed that son of a bitch into the middle of the desert. I don't reckon that anyone ever found it again. The earth is full of evil things. I don't think I was naive to add something evil back into its soil.

I believe that was my first encounter with a haunted object. I'd love to go back to the 20 year old me, a scared kid trying to do right by his parents, and tell him that he'd grow up to be a paranormal cremator. But on second thought, I think he'd just laugh in my face. Hell, he'd probably hit me.

I'm far too old to take a punch these days.

After the war, I met Norma right after I returned home to Boone, NC. We got married and had two years together before she complained about a headache one summer afternoon in 48' and died in her sleep. The doctors said it was natural, but I'll always wonder if that wasn't the case. I'm old and forgetful now, but I still think about Norma every single day. It don't hurt like it used to, but it don't feel good neither.

Between the way my white neighbors treated me and the loss of Norma, I didn't care too much for people at the time, so I looked to find work where I had as little contact with folks as I could and I ended up chasing a help wanted ad in the local paper. I don't remember if the particulars of the job were even listed. It just promised a steady wage and some solitary labor and that's all I wanted. I caught a bus to a little town outside of Wilkesboro where I met Benton Fisk, the owner of the Fisk Crematorium. He sized me up real good that morning because I think he expected someone older. He probably thought I was there to play him for a fool, but it didn't take long for Benton to see that I was hardworking, trustworthy and just wanted to be left alone. I think Benton and I were similar that way.

I spent months sleeping on a cot in the attic of the crematorium while Benton taught me the trade. He was too old to move the bodies so I mostly helped with that, but I took a liking to the job pretty quick and

Benton took a liking to me. Considering how much death I had seen in the War, I found something peaceful in the work. Benton told me that people have been performing cremations for 17,000 years. After a while, I started to wonder why we even put our loved ones in the earth whole.

Ashes to ashes, dust to dust, as they say.

One night, I couldn't sleep on account of a nightmare I had about Norma and I could hear Benton enter the crematorium at some ungodly hour. I snuck down the attic stairs and watched as he opened a small burlap sack and tossed a mason jar into the furnace. I found it an awfully odd sight, so I tried my best to get back to sleep, but the next day I said to him,

"What were you doing here last night?"

He just looked at me and said, "Wallace, you sure have been a blessing, but you ain't ready yet."

I had no idea what that meant and I didn't feel like pressing on his nerves, so I kept my head down and focused on moving bodies to the retort, packaging the ashes, and preparing the urns. A few weeks went by, but it wasn't long before I woke, once again, to find Benton by the furnace with a candle in his hand, struggling to put something inside it. I was worried the old man was liable to throw out his back so I rushed over and told him, "Let me help you with that."

Startled, he dropped the bag and a ceramic flower vase about two feet tall rolled onto the floor. I went to pick it up and Benton screamed at me something fierce,

"Don't touch that!"

He was madder than a puffed toad and just as ugly, but I think it was because he was scared. It took him a minute to catch his breath but he eventually got the vase into the furnace, closed its door, and went into the kitchen to put a kettle on.

"Let me tell you what I really do here," he said to me. There's a long story here and probably a short one too.

Either way, they're both strange.

It turned out that Benton moonlighted as something he called a "paranormal cremator," and the flower vase had once belonged to a family in Cork, Ireland. Somehow, it had travelled all the way to the Fisk Crematorium to be disposed of.

"That vase you almost touched was responsible for nothing but misery and death. It was cursed," he said.

I guess folks all across the world heard about Benton and knew what he did. In a way, he was famous. People would bring him all sorts of stuff to burn and bury.

"The dark secret is that it's not people or places who take the effects of evil," he said. "It's things, Wallace. Things."

"Why can't them folks just burn the objects themselves?" I asked.

Benton told me that he practiced ancient rituals which rendered his furnace unique amongst all the other furnaces on Earth. He said he'd teach me all about it if I wouldn't run off scared. I hadn't run from much in my life and didn't plan on starting anytime soon, so I talked the old man into learning me his second trade, one where I'd be helping rid the world of evil things. I thought of Beau and hoped he was doing ok, then I thought about that silver ring.

That night, I didn't sleep very well.

———————

BENTON STORED a leather physicians bag in a closet of the crematorium. I had seen it with my own eyes many times and never thought twice about it, but it wasn't long before he opened it up and showed me what was inside. The bag held a few vials of salt, some chalk, and a few slips of some parchment paper, That's it. He taught me how to draw warding insignias for an order that has no name, but has been protecting humanity from haunted objects since Perdikkas ruled Greece. The symbols contained combinations of circles and triangles that formed the shapes of what I thought looked like flowers.

"Draw this one to protect yourself, draw this one to protect others, and draw this one to protect the furnace," he said to me.

Benton had a shelf of books on world history in the attic and let me tell you what, considering all the time I spent alone, I often didn't feel that way diving into all of them books. He told me that every single conflict in history was a direct cause of some haunted object. I don't reckon I believe all of that, but I sure found it interesting and my thirst for understanding grew with every single page I read. During the day I burned bodies, but at night, I helped Benton burn everything from shoes, to paintings, to jewelry.

"Have any of these things ever caused you harm? " I asked him one night while we loaded the furnace with a child's train set. Benton just stared into the fire, his eyes glowing like embers.

"No," he said. His mind was elsewhere. "But that does not change the reason why we do what we do."

Eventually, I stopped asking why the folks brought us the items. The stories were almost always the same. The object came into the person's life and a chain of bad things soon followed. People got sick. People got killed or killed themselves. Rich people went poor. Poor people got worse off.

"We're here to break the chains," Benton said.

I liked the idea of that. It made me feel like I was doing something good for the world even if I questioned if some of the objects needed the pageantry of a magical send off. If anything, we were giving people peace of mind and that was enough to keep me doing it long after Benton passed from a cancer in his lungs. He left me the crematorium, his cottage, and his Chevy pickup truck in his will and testament with a simple note.

"In flames, we trust," it said.

Teddy is the first object I can ever remember being left on the doorstep of the Fisk Crematorium. I always exchanged letters with clients and they travelled here to make the drop off. That was one of Benton's most sacred rules. Or, I guess that was one of the Order's most sacred rules. Every object had to be hand delivered by its owner. Once the item crossed the threshold, it needed to be burned immediately. That was another sacred rule. I woke up one morning and when I arrived at Fisks, Teddy was just lying there, smiling up at me, a little, brown teddy bear with black button eyes, a black button nose, and a red ribbon around its neck. I took one look at it and for some reason the bear reminded me of Norma. I kept every single promise that I ever made to Benton. That is, until the day I met Teddy.

I told myself that the bear wasn't haunted. I figured a grieving family dropped it off as a gesture of goodwill, so I picked Teddy up off the ground and brought him inside. I sat him in a chair and told him,

"Teddy, I'm Wallace. It's nice to meet you."

I reckon how crazy this may sound, but I was lonely. I had recently hired an apprentice named Tony to help out with the day to day tasks at the crematorium, but I wasn't convinced he was ready for the other trade.

Not yet, anyway.

Well, I told Teddy all about my day. I told him about what I was reading, I played Muddy Waters records for him, hell, on that first day I treated Teddy like he was my best friend and it felt right, even though I felt ashamed I was talking to a stuffed animal like some sort of crackpot. That night, I drove Teddy back to my cottage and fell asleep with him in my arms, pretending it was Norma.

When I woke up the next day, I realized I had made a mistake.

First of all, Teddy wasn't in the bed with me. I got up confused, expecting to wish him a good morning, but came out of my bedroom to find him sitting on the living room sofa. The front door of the cottage was wide open and there was an index finger lying in a pool of dried blood on the threshold.

"Did you do this, Teddy?" I asked, as if I was expecting the damned stuffed animal to answer me. I was still in my pajamas when I got to Fisk's that morning, but instead of tossing Teddy in the furnace, I grabbed the chalk, drew a ward to protect myself, and burned the finger. Tony arrived shortly after that and looked at me all kinds of strange.

I don't blame him.

"Teddy, I don't want you doing anything like that ever again," I said, going on about my day like everything was okay. I hate to say it, but Teddy was the only thing I had. I let Tony take the reins at Fisks and brought Teddy to the park. We sat on a bench together feeding birds and I told him all about Norma.

That night, I made sure to lock the door.

I WOKE up the next day and everything seemed fine. I brought Teddy to Fisk's and went upstairs. I was beginning to think the entire unpleasantness was a dream. Tony arrived and we went about our day as usual but it didn't take long for all hell to break loose.

"I'm going to head out to lunch," Tony said around noon.

I was resting in a chair in the parlor and Teddy was sitting next to me. I nodded at Tony and he turned around to leave. That's when I saw Teddy move. He got up off that chair and ran towards Tony like Jesse Owens. His furry little arms swung back and forth and there was this little pitter patter sound as his legs swiped across the floor. I tried to warn Tony, but I didn't have time. He turned around to say one more thing to me and it was too late. Teddy was on him. I watched in horror as that little stuffed animal climbed up his legs and worked up to his neck. Tony's eyes bugged out of his skull in shock and I got up to go over and help him, but I'm too old, and too slow. Before I had even gotten out of the chair, I heard a wet snapping sound and Tony's neck had been wrung into a shape that reminded me of the chickens my Dad would take care of when I was a kid. As soon as Tony hit the floor, Teddy lay there, seemingly lifeless again.

I'm sorry, but I didn't put Teddy in that furnace. I

put Tony in there instead and went home crying like the day Norma died.

TIME IS A FUNNY THING. I wake up some days thinking today is the day I'm gonna get shot down in a plane, but then I try to get out of bed and remember that I'm just old and wrinkled. I don't know where that time went, but I've seen enough to know that this world ain't ever gonna change.

A BLOODY HEIST

The pipe bomb detonates as a woman in a luchador mask resembling El Santo takes a swig from a stainless steel flask. It's what she needs to stave off the shakes. She sits cross legged in the back of a stolen U-Haul truck approximately seventeen miles away from the explosion.

"Got any left?" Mr. Barlow asks from across the floor.

"That was the last of it. An '87 red."

"A good year," Dracula says while monitoring a local news feed on his smartphone. A police scanner buzzes furiously with activity. They can overhear law enforcement dispatching state and local police officers to Monument Avenue, the site where Nosferatu planted the second device at 4:00 am. Two days ago, their first bomb killed or critically injured 300 people in Arlington. The four vampire masked criminals wait in the parking lot of a Wawa in Ashland, VA. The events unfolding have been planned with a meticulous attention to detail. They know the routes; they know agent response times.

"How many?" El Santo asks.

"Thanks to the half marathon, a lot," Dracula says as the sirens of emergency vehicles and first responders whine past them towards I-95 S.

"I've got eyes on our truck," Mr. Barlow says, peering down at a tablet that feeds them a live view from a DJi Phantom drone. The bird's eye shot hovers over an armored truck in Henrico County heading north towards Northern Virginia. Like clockwork, the departure time they anticipated is exact.

Fifteen minutes until interception.

"Thanks to Mark 1, they were flooded with donations," Dracula says, cleaning the pieces of a long barreled assault rifle. "This score will be able to feed our people for years."

"Looks like Mark 2 did its job. The heat is moving south," Mr. Barlow says.

El Santo wraps the creases of her tactical gear in dark, reflective tape and taps her chest to make sure she is wearing her Kevlar vest. She did not forget. This is her first outing with the crew and for some reason she is shaken by the images displayed on the news coverage. It's a blunt depiction of their work: visceral shots of blood stained asphalt and severed limbs lying across the awnings of outdoor restaurants. People in shock with their hands on their hips, struggling to hold back tears. She has hurt people many, many times before, but never a large group of presumably innocent bystanders.

"Do you feel bad for their families?" she asks the gang.

The masks of Dracula and Mr. Barlow glance at the floor. Nosferatu, the architect, chimes in to break the awkward silence.

"El Santo, I welcome your feelings of empathy and counter your query with this: do they feel bad for us?"

She thinks for a moment, but has no answer.

Nosferatu continues.

"They took away our health care. They wrote legislation to label us terrorists and that whole time, none of *them* said a word. None of *them* moved an inch to help us as we were systematically hunted and forced to hide in the shadows like animals. They don't give a flying fuck about you, or any of us."

Dracula slams an extended clip into his rifle with gusto.

"They let my wife and children burn the same day that Senator Cruise called us a vile drain on American society," he says.

Mr. Barlow puts down the tablet and exposes his right forearm which is covered in scar tissue.

"An agent laughed in my face while he did this to me. Don't forget while you're here today. Lestat wasn't so lucky."

El Santo reads them loud and clear. Their mission reflects an unfortunate reality. The gang has options, but Nosferatu's plan is the one that will keep them from being exposed.

They are starving. Success will keep them alive long enough to plan their next set of moves.

"It's time. Make sure you're covered," Nosferatu says. He pounds on a thick steel plate that has been welded to the interior of the truck for good luck. Dracula lifts the latch and Nosferatu exits. A moment passes before El Santo, Dracula, and Mr. Barlow hear the engine roar to life. The truck exits the parking lot of the Wawa and wastes no time merging onto the on ramp of I-95 N. Traffic is light. Mr. Barlow continues to monitor the armored truck with the drone. They're moving north, approaching exit 95-B when the armored truck moves into view behind them. Nosferatu slows the U-Haul down in the right lane and goads the armored truck into passing them.

"Now," Nosferatu says over a walkie talkie.

Dracula, Mr. Barlow, and El Santo brace themselves.

When the armored truck is parallel to the U-Haul, Mr. Barlow throws a switch while Nosferatu side-swipes their vehicle into the broad side of the armored truck. The steel plates that have been welded into the frame of the U-Haul are connected to a large, powerful electromagnet. Prior to his life on the run, Mr. Barlow was a world renowned electrical engineer. When

Nosferatu rams into the side of the armored truck, it sticks to the side of the U-Haul like a fly caught in a strip of glue paper. He can see the driver frantically trying to hit the brakes and change directions, but the agents are stuck. The stolen rental truck slows down from the added weight while Nosferatu pulls off of the road and moves them underneath a large two lane overpass. This gives them enough shade to complete their job.

Dracula exits the back of the U-Haul with his assault rifle in hand. He places a small explosive on the driver side door of the armored truck and takes three steps backwards. On the interior, Mr. Barlow presses a switch. A small explosion rings out underneath the overpass. The gang spent months perfecting this device using gender reveal celebrations as cover for their tests. The door comes ajar and the driver of the armored truck bleeds from the concussion of the explosion. The agent in the passenger seat can not exit as his door is stuck to the side of the U-Haul. He attempts to draw a handgun and fire it at Dracula, but the man behind the mask was once a military marksman. Within seconds, Dracula has fired four shots from his rifle at close range. Two to the head, two to the chest. Both agents slump over in their seats, dead. Mr. Barlow and El Santo hop out of the truck as Dracula prepares another explosive device. Nosferatu checks a stopwatch. Fifty-three seconds have passed since he pulled off the highway.

They are working together like a well oiled machine.

The next explosion blows open the hatch of the armored truck. An unmarked white van sits parked under the overpass. Nosferatu unlocks it and enters the driver side door as El Santo, Dracula, and Mr. Barlow enter the back of the armored truck. Nosferatu backs up the vehicle and within a minute, the team has moved 12 large, black duffel bags inside the van. The police scanner can still be heard in the background. The dispatcher continues to order units to the site of the pipe bomb explosion. El Santo takes over the steering wheel of the white van.

The getaway is her moment.

The gang enters and she peels off, rips the wheels into a sharp turn, and hits the exit back towards the southbound lane. They exit 95, hit 54, then 301. In 15 minutes they are back home in the middle of nowhere, an abandoned warehouse in Bowling Green, VA.

THE DUFFEL BAGS sit on a large table, stacked on top of one another. The dark room is lit by a few candles. Hours have passed since the heist and as political pundits on media channels decry the violence from the Richmond Marathon bombing, Nosferatu,

Mr. Barlow, Dracula, and El Santo sit around the table.

They remove their masks.

Nosferatu zips open a duffel bag and removes a pint from the cache. A pint of blood, donated by folks who rushed to do their part after the first explosion in Arlington.

The four gang members smile, their fangs glistening in the night. Around them, hundreds of fangs smile alongside them.

It is time to eat.

HOURGLASS

"Jerry, I apologize. I know this is your first sacrifice with us, but I promise that we usually get this right," Bill says. A young man bound to a chair screams into a thick layer of duct tape wrapped around his mouth. In the darkness of a two car garage, four middle aged men look at the floor. They count a set of burning candles at their feet.

"How many candles are we supposed to have here?" Chip says.

"Seven?" Kenny says, unsure of his answer. He pulls up his black theatre mask so he can see the floor better. There is an ominous symbol marked across the cement by a few pieces of black electrical tape. Two equilateral triangles whose points meet in the center of a recognizable shape:

It's an hourglass.

The man in the chair continues to scream as blood

drips from a gash in his forehead. Chip holds a set of garden snips.

"No, no no," Bill, an accountant, says. His math is never wrong. "It's six for chickens, seven for goats, and eight for humans."

Chip, the silver haired cult leader, retrieves an ancient scroll from a small toolbox in the garage. He checks to make sure they have followed the correct protocol.

"Bill is right. We should have eight."

The men burst into laughter.

"Seven! You're not a goat, are you?" Kenny says, leaning into the face of the man in the chair. His breath is putrid, reeking from the three day old pot roast stuck between his dentures. The man in the chair has stopped screaming. There is no longer a point. Kenny hands their new recruit, Jerry, a candle and a stick lighter.

"Here you go. Knock yourself out," he says. Jerry lights the candle and completes the semi-circle.

Now, the ceremony can proceed.

"At my command, state your wish," Chip says while holding a small, bronze goblet up to the head wound of the man in the chair. It isn't bleeding enough, so he goes back to work with the snips.

"Colleen has been gunning for the PTO presidency for six months. I say it's time we take down that bitch Marge Lansky," Kenny says. The men raise their arms in unison and hum a steady low pitched note.

"I want Brett's lacrosse team to win a state title this year. Go Trojans," Bill says. The men continue to hum while Chip fills the cup from the wound. Now, it gushes fresh blood. Some of it makes it into the cup, some of it hits the unfinished floor of the garage. The man in the chair whimpers, but his blood and sweat have mixed together causing the duct tape around his wrists to loosen. He carefully pulls and twists his hands behind his back.

"I've always wanted an in ground pool," Jerry says. The other men smile at him, as if to say *great wish*.

You'll fit in here just fine, Jerry.

They hum.

"Golzar, I request with your blessing, a new set of Calloway clubs," Chip says.

A light in the garage turns on, revealing the men and their work. They look at each other in momentary panic as a woman's voice calls into the room.

"Chip, what is going on in here?" She says. The man in the chair stiffens his posture, hopeful for a rescue.

Jerry is about to push the button to open the garage door and flee, when he sees a woman in an apron standing in the light. A halo is cast over a set of blonde curls and a pearl necklace.

It is Chip's wife, Karen.

"We can't host a sacrifice if our guests aren't properly fed. Who wants muffins?" she asks, raising a silver tray into the air. The smell of blueberries wafts into the garage, mixing with the smell of blood, grass, and gasoline. The man in the chair screams, again. The men take turns grabbing muffins and scarf them down. Nothing whets the appetite like an old fashioned sacrifice.

"These are so moist," Kenny says while his lips smack together.

"Are these gluten-free?" Jerry asks. "I'm seriously allergic to gluten." Bill puts his hand up to get Karen's attention as he swallows.

"Karen, you'll never believe it. We only put out seven candles," he says. Karen smiles and locks eyes with the young man in the chair.

"Seven candles. Ha. You're not a goat, are you?"

They bleat at the man in the chair. Chip puts his fingers up to his head to make horns and shakes it side to side like a goat.

"I love you, honey," he says.

"I love you, too," Karen says, giving him a kiss before she heads back inside the home with the empty serving tray. The light goes out and Chip raises the goblet full of blood into the air.

"Now that our bodies have been nourished. Let us drink, and may Golzar fulfill your desires," he says. He passes the cup to Jerry, who gulps down the blood as if he's shotgunning a beer on the back nine.

"Whoa, Jerry, slow down. A sip is fine," Bill says. Jerry burps.

"Sorry fellas."

The man in the chair continues to wrench his hands back and forth. The men pass the cup around their cult of accountants, lawyers, and doctors. Chip looks over at a small table behind Kenny.

"Bring forth the hourglass," he says, pointing to the object which rests on a beautiful sheet of purple felt. It is two feet tall and filled with fine grains of sand. As Kenny goes to pick it up, he trips over an extension cord and knocks it down onto the cement floor. The glass shatters, the sand spilling across their feet.

"I am so sorry," he says, enraging Bill.

"Dammit Kenny, how are we going to open the void now?"

"Call Chet, he has a spare," Chip says.

"I'm on it," Kenny says picking up his smartphone. He disappears into the house. Jerry breaks the tension.

"So, does Greenfields take part in the dance ritual?

Chip smiles and slides his mask back down.

"Oh, Jerry, we dance. We dance."

Chip, Bill, and Jerry undulate their bodies in a coordinated set of movements to a song that only they can hear. Jerry wipes the blood that runs down his chin and licks his fingers clean. Bill looks up at the ceiling of the garage and howls like a werewolf. The three men are in a trance and speaking in tongues when the man in the chair frees himself. The captors are so lost in their annual ceremony that it's only when Chip glances down at the chair again, he realizes it is empty.

The man is gone.

HE SHAMBLES down the middle of the street in a cul-de-sac. Sunlight pierces his eyes as they adjust to what is a beautiful afternoon. Surrounded by an idyllic set of model homes, he hears the sounds of sprinklers spraying water across perfectly manicured lawns. American flags rustle in the wind. He props himself up on a white pickett fence, leaving behind a smear of blood as a BMW turns on to the street. The man flags it down and rushes over to the passenger side door. The driver lowers the window.

"What's going on, are you okay?" the driver asks.

"Where am I?"

"What do you mean? This is Greenfields."

"Please, you've got to help me. I've been trapped in a garage for days with some sort of cult. They're trying to kill me," he says.

"Quick, get in the car, you'll be safe with me."

The car locks click open, allowing the man to enter the back seat of the luxury car. He collapses in exhaustion, closes his eyes and whispers words of thanks. When he opens them again, he looks into the rearview mirror and notices the crooked smile of the driver. Then, he sees it sitting next to him in the empty seat.

It's the spare hourglass.

THE OLD BAY KING

"I was born on the shores of the Chesapeake Bay
But Maryland and Virginia have faded away
And I keep thinking tomorrow is coming today
So I am endlessly waiting"
-Counting Crows

"We're crab people now"
-Charlie Kelly

"It's one of those bastard crabs!"
-Guy N. Smith

I apologize if this doesn't make much sense, but I don't have much time left and the battery of my phone died a while ago. I've broken a few bones before: my radius, ulna, left ankle, and a pair of ribs, but my personal experience with blood loss had been nonexistent, apart from some scrapes and scratches, until that damn box opened.

That's rare for a crabber.

Now, I can barely see, I'm tired as hell, and I can feel my heart pounding like a clydesdale on the inside of my chest. When this adrenaline wears off I don't know if I'll survive. There is a seven inch gash, a quarter of an inch deep, down the middle of my back. The damn thing missed my spine by a few millimeters. I can still walk, but I don't have nowhere to go and I've been focusing on getting the bleeding to stop so I can let you know what happened to us. I'm marooned on The Fiddler, likely a few miles east of Dagsboro, but I lost track of time hours ago, days even.

Dan is dead. His body is starting to change colors and I'd cry but it may hear me. I'm laid up in a cabinet behind him in the crew room while a bunch of Jimmies that escaped their holds scuttle nearby. At this point there's hundreds of them slipping in through a hole in the door left by Dan's shotgun blast. I have a feeling they're starting to think that Dan looks tasty. Hell, if someone doesn't find me soon I'll be in the stomachs of a few thousand blue crabs myself. I can't say I blame them.

That was the whole point of this weekend: crabs.

You see, Dan and I started crabbing in 2008 but the banks wouldn't loan either of us money, so we did what we had to do, which means that we took money from Otis Bailey, the "Old Bay King."

If you go up to the seafood counter in any supermarket in Delaware, Maryland, or Virgina, you've probably seen the Bailey Foods logo. You might even speak highly of their blue crab meat. That's what most people think of when they think of Otis. But in our neck of the woods, Otis is known for pushing oxy, and Dan loved oxy. I should have known better than to get involved in a business with someone that couldn't go an hour without swallowing a handful of pills, but Dan was my best friend long before his addiction and I certainly wasn't going anywhere in life working seventy hours a week at the stop and shop. The two of us spent most of the weekends of our childhood together crabbing, so I figured why the hell not.

The first few years of our partnership went great. I was able to buy my own trailer on a nice lot of land, I met Tina, and we had Abby. Dan cut back on the pills and Otis never seemed to mind that we were out there hauling in crabs. I mean, we were never going to compete with his fleet of ships all across the waters of Maryland, so as long as our envelopes of cash with the 30% interest on top made it to his goons, we were out of sight and out of mind.

We were about two years away from finishing our

loan when the crab shortages hit. When Otis's bottom line started to take a nosedive, he stopped being friendly. He pushed our monthly payments up by 10, then 15, then 20 percent and when we couldn't make them anymore, he started shaking us down in a bad way. He had a guy named Clark break a few of Dan's fingers and another guy showed up to my trailer one night and stared me up and down while pointing to the open trunk of his Buick. Then, last week, Otis showed up as we were prepping The Fiddler for our most important trip out on the Bay. This was the haul that we needed to keep our business afloat. Our lives, too.

Otis complicated things. He approached us in athletic sandals, basketball shorts, and black track jacket - the complete and opposite attire you'd think a multi-millionaire kingpin would choose to wear. He was in his 60s, balding, and slightly overweight, but I'll be honest, he scared the shit out of me.

"If you boys are off to score some sooks, you best stay south of Cedar Island," he said to us, smiling while sucking in his spit through his front teeth. He had a pair of guys at the top of the dock sitting in a beige sedan, and he had clearly instructed them to hang back. "My crews haven't had any luck in days."

"Thank you, Mr. Bailey," Dan said, tossing the last of one of our smaller traps onto the deck of The Fiddler. When Dan turned around, Otis was on him like a pitbull. He grabbed him by his throat and pinned him down onto the boards of the dock as I put up my hands to make sure he was clear I wasn't a threat.

"Don't you dare thank me for anything right now, you cocksuckers. Y'all are five months late and if none of my crews can find crab, and that's the way y'all are hoping to make ends meet, how the fuck is this arrangement going to work out for me?"

Dan went to answer, but Otis smashed his fist into his lips before he had the chance to respond.

"Shut the fuck up, son. I'm coming out to check up on y'all mid-week. If your holds aren't full to the brim, we're going to kill you, dump you in the bay, and then we're gonna kill your families for fun. Do you understand?" He said, wiping Dan's blood off of his knuckles with a handkerchief that he pulled out from one of the pockets of his track jacket.

"Yes, sir," Dan said.

I nodded.

After Otis threatened Abby's life I stood there seething and watched him casually walk back up the dock before being driven away. Dan licked his wounds while we finished getting the boat ready. It was a little unusual to head out as a pair, but we had to lay off our usual crew thanks to the crab shortages. This was going to be like old times. Both of us were scared, but neither one of us admitted it to each other.

The first couple of days went like any: we left Kilmarnock and spent hours dropping and baiting pots down to Poquoson. We didn't speak a word about Otis.

We took separate shifts sleeping as we headed east towards Smith Island, when one morning out of the blue Dan just up and lost his mind.

"You know what? Fuck Otis, Let's head north," he said. I could hear the bottle of pills rattling around in his coat pocket.

I tried to reason with him, but after twenty years of friendship you know when to pick and choose your battles and I could tell this wasn't the right time to argue with Dan. Eventually I agreed to move north, provided that we'd grab some additional fuel at some point so we could chart south like we had originally intended. It really didn't matter where we went. That whole season the crabs had stopped biting.

That is, until the storm hit.

I think it was last Tuesday. We had kept a steady eye on all of the forecasts before departing Kilmarnock and that morning our radar had nothing odd to report, but around one o'clock in the afternoon we got to smelling thunder. If you've been out on the water long enough, you can instantly recognize that smell. It's sweet, like the nectar of a Sweetbay. It happened so fast I'm having trouble thinking of how to explain what happened. One minute we were pulling up empty traps and the next we were fending off some of the choppiest waters I've ever navigated. To make matters worse, the sun was gone and we were left to fend for ourselves in near total darkness. The Fiddler was probably pitched up at a seventy degree angle from a series of massive waves when I started to pray and I hadn't done that in a very, very long time. The storm only lasted ten minutes, but it felt like a year. Then, it was over.

Dan and I started laughing something fierce because I think we both thought it over right then and there, but as soon as the storm broke Jimmies started circling our boat. I mean, thousands of them. I've never seen so many fuckin crabs before in my life. It's like they were searching us out, calling to us. I could hear them clicking in the water even though I was standing way up at the helm. We ditched the traps all together and dropped our trawling net and in less than an hour we filled every single hold of The Fiddler. At that moment, I truly believe God had answered my prayers. I was about to give Dan a big ol' hug when I caught him staring into the horizon.

"What is that?" He asked. My eyesight isn't so good, so I fished out my binoculars and about a thousand yards to our east I caught a glimpse of a derelict riverboat. It looked like something straight out of a Mark Twain novel. The damn thing had a steam engine and everything. Dan shook his head in disbelief. I asked what something like that was doing sitting there a few miles off of the Atlantic coast, but Dan certainly didn't have an answer. Even from that distance, we knew it was a ghost ship. There was no visible evidence anyone was on board, but we decided to go take a gander anyway just to be sure, so we dropped anchor beside it and put out a call on the radio to which no one responded.

It didn't take Dan much of a debate to decide who would hop onto the deck of the riverboat first. He pretty much volunteered himself. We grabbed a pair of flashlights, a flare, and I'm pretty sure he grabbed his snub nose too before crossing onto the boat, which didn't have a name as far as we could tell. All across the wooden railings the paint was rotting away like dead skin. Its metal beams were coated in a thick layer of rust and there was an inescapable odor of brine and seaweed everywhere. It gave me the creeps. We walked throughout the first deck back to back looking for signs of life, trying to piece together the mystery of what happened. The ship had been emptied out. There was no furniture, no earthly possessions, and no food or cooking utensils left in the kitchen. We were truly walking through a skeleton, our flashlights reflecting off of the bones of an artifact from the Victorian age. The second deck, just like the first, was empty stern to bow as well.

We climbed the exterior steps to get up to the third and final deck, but when we tried head inside we discovered that the doors had been locked from the inside. We tried looking through the windows, but they had been covered by layers of old, yellow sheets of newspaper. The articles ranged in dates from 1885 to 1888. At this point, I told Dan we should leave. I said our holds were full and we could get in touch with Otis to set things straight, but before I had finished my plea he smashed one of the windows with the strong end of his flashlight and started shimmying his way through it. I sat in defeat with my back against the exterior deck wall waiting for him to come out, but as soon as he hit the ground inside, he started screaming.

"Lord, Lord help me," he said, his breath erratic. I didn't want to cut myself on the broken glass, so I poked my head through the window and brought my flashlight up to find Dan laying on a large pile of human bones. There were thousands of them scattered across the floor.

Clean, white, bones.

Some of them had been broken into smaller, jagged pieces. Some of them were connected to ominous shapes that still resembled something human, but I'd guess that we had stumbled upon the remains of some-where between seventy five and one hundred people. Some of the skeletons were small. Young. I gagged while thinking about the horror that took place at some point in this room. I wished at that moment that Dan had listened to me when I said we should leave, but that asshole never listened to me. I was about to turn around and head back to The Fiddler when my flash-light reflected off of something strange in the center of the room about fifteen feet away from the two of us. Dan saw it too. The beams of our flashlights slowly brought the shape into view as the light hit its sides.

"Is that, is that?..." Dan's voice trailed off.

In the center of the third deck, in the middle of all of this death and decay, laid a rectangular box that was clearly made of solid gold.

Look, Dan and I might have been a few sausages short of a BBQ, but seeing that box did more than just pique our curiosity. I think we both felt like we hit the lottery. Yes, the damn thing was in the middle of a room littered with human remains, but as we got closer to it and confirmed that it was indeed a six foot long, 3 foot tall, and 3 foot wide box made of gold, I think we both nearly passed out. It was covered with a series of ornate etchings from a language neither of us spoke. It was truly the most beautiful thing I had ever seen. It didn't take us long to start to formulate a plan on how to move the box to The Fiddler.

We kept a pair of raise-n-roll, manual hydraulic jacks on hand for moving traps to our holds and those things have a max capacity of 4000 lbs. We giggled like little kids wheeling those jacks into that room, kicking aside bones and discussing the logistics of how and where we could safely melt this box down into a form of currency that would end our needs for money, forever. Can you imagine that?

No bills.

No debt.

Sleeping in?

I've worked my ass off every single day of my life. I liked the idea of being lazy for once. Anyway, we estimated with some armchair mathematics that it was probably worth somewhere between ten to twelve million dollars. Hallelujah, indeed.

Dan grabbed the left jack and I took the right. We were amazed to find that our gear lifted it right up without too much trouble. We carefully wheeled the box down the wooden planks of the riverboat and placed it down onto a timber pallet at the stern of its third deck. Dan took charge of The Fiddler's crane and dropped its line down so I could suspend the steel wire through the bottom of the pallet. We were nervous, but after some careful planning it only took about an hour of labor to get the golden box safely onto the deck of The Fiddler. We covered it with a blue tarp and some elastic bungee cords and set our coordinates for Dagsboro. We were so wrapped up in the daydream of wealth that we didn't even look back as the riverboat disappeared in the waters behind us. A flock of seagulls circled around our heads, cawing, when Dan smiled at me.

"And, we still got our crabs for Otis," he said, proudly.

Shit, at that point I had forgotten all about Otis.

My Mama always told me that when you speak of the Devil he tends to hear it and I shit you not, right after Dan brought up the crabs, our dispatch radio went off and it was Otis ready to come out and verify that we'd be able to make good on our payment.

"I thought I told you to go south?" he said, when we gave him our location.

We didn't mention our detour.

"You'll be happy. I promise," Dan said.

"Yeah, yeah. I better be for both of y'alls sake. We're actually not far from there. Be there shortly. Stay put." He replied before disconnecting from the radio.

It felt like only a few seconds had passed before we heard the buzzing engine of a Bayliner speeding towards us. Dan and I stood there watching Otis, Clark, and some other goon in a black three piece suit aggressively approach our ship. We hoped that he would see the holds full of blue crab and then let us get on our merry way, but that was probably naive of us.

They climbed on board and let the awkward silence marinate for a bit so I stewed in the anxiety. Clark cradled a pump action shotgun like it was a newborn baby. I'm pretty sure the other guy was armed too, but he wasn't quite as obvious about it.

"Pat them down, boys," Otis said. The muscle obeyed his orders and gave us a quick search. I was right about my hunch from earlier. The suited man retrieved Dan's snubnose from the waist of his jeans. Clark motioned the tip of his shotgun to direct us towards the crab holds. We kept our hands up, even though we had just been checked.

"Alright, let's see it," Otis said. I think he was excited at the prospect of finding them empty. I don't think he minded getting blood on his hands very much, but we opened the top of the hold chamber to show off our miraculous catch.

"Here. A full load," Dan said, while the bounty of crabs clicked in a symphony that any fisherman worthy of their salt knows well. It's the sound of money.

"Well, well, well. I must say, I'm a bit curious how y'all made it happen fellas, but I'm a man of my word and that's a nice set of bushels, so why don't you all head over to Hampton and drop them off with my crew. It's easy to find since it's the biggest crab plant on the east coast," his muscle started laughing in order to appease their master.

"Sure thing," Dan said.

Now, normally this would have set Dan off because our haul was easily worth three times what we owed Otis, so really, he was robbing us blind, but we needed to get him the fuck off our boat. We wanted this interaction to be our last with the Old Bay King.

You know what they say about shit and how fast it moves downhill?

Well, I imagine they were just about to leave, but for some cursed reason the goon in the black suit saw the tarp and got nosy.

"What's in there?" He asked. Dan tried telling him it was a stack of empty pots but Clark walked over to it and nudged the edge of the tarp with the end of his Shotgun. I could tell he realized what it was by the tone of his voice when he said

"Boss, come take a look at this."

Before we knew it, Otis and his goons had popped off the bungee cords and revealed the large golden box underneath. At that point, I knew we were as good as dead.

"Is that gold?" Clark asked, dumbfounded. Otis started licking his chops. He saw the end of his financial troubles, just like we had before him. He laughed, maniacally.

"Oh my, my. No wonder you boys didn't mind me taking your catch. You thought you could pull a fast one on me? Where exactly did you find this?"

Dan told him about the riverboat, I guess hoping that the story would help save our hides. I kept my head down. I knew what was coming. I started to pray again.

"Sounds like we got us a pair of Jim Hawkin's boys," he said with his hands on his belly. I was expecting to find my ass in the drink any second, when I heard the blast of a shotgun. I felt the sensation of hot blood splatter across my face and when I opened my eyes from prayer, I saw the smoking barrel of Clark's shotgun a few inches away from Otis, who no longer had a head. His neck spewed blood into the air so loudly I could hear it gurgling up through the arteries of his neck like a geyser. He collapsed to his knees, falling into a smear that had once been his face, skull, and brain. I could see that his blood had sprayed all over the surface of the golden box.

"Dump his body in the water. Now," the suited man commanded. With a shotgun and a snub nosed pistol aimed at us, we didn't put up much of a fight. We dragged his dead body to the edge of the deck, flipped it over the rail, and watched Otis's headless corpse rag doll into the Atlantic Ocean.

Good riddance.

"Here's what's going to happen. Y'all are going to navigate us to the docks in Kilmarnock. The way I see it, your debt with Otis is done. You can keep the catch, but this box is ours. If you try anything funny, we'll kill you," Clark said. While he spoke, I saw the man in the suit point to the box.

"What is happening?" He asked.

The blood that had splattered onto the box started moving. It collected into a small pool, which began to run down the etchings of the strange, mysterious language which covered its lid. Then, the blood disappeared. It appeared like the box was drinking it.

"What....the...fuck," Dan said.

Ok, this is why I apologized back at the start. This is where things are a little hazy and hard for me to explain, even compared to the rest of this mess. When the blood disappeared, the lid of the box started shifting. It almost appeared mechanical. The gold started to give way to a small opening, which gradually grew wider and wider until the lid disappeared all together.

After a few seconds, something emerged from the box.

It was alive and straight out of the nightmares I had as a child growing up on the Rappahannock. It was probably just under six feet tall like the length of the box, and it was thin, red, and covered in barnacles. It looked like an insect, but it walked upright like a praying mantis. It had two clawed arms above something thorax-like and then two smaller ones below it that were bladed.

Clark took one look at it before he pumped the shotgun and readied a shot, but the thing in the box was fast and it was agile. It took one leap before it used its bladed appendages to sever Clarks right arm in one graceful motion. Before the arm and his shotgun hit the ground, I watched the thing lift Clark into the air with its claws, effortlessly. One set grasped him at his clavicle, the other set wrapped around his midsection. They pinched together like a vice grip and turned Clark into three sections of meat. I heard him snap like a Crab's leg on the 4th of July as his entrails spilled all over the deck of The Fiddler.

I started to run towards the crew room as the man in the black suit fired hopeless shots from the snub nose pistol at the creature. I yelled for Dan to grab the shotgun as the suited man screamed something awful. We were climbing up the stairs towards the crew room when I heard wings and the unmistakable hiss of a pissed off cockroach. The damn thing could fly. I was about to hit the crew room entrance when the thing dropped down from the air right in front of me.

I gazed directly into its eyes, two little lifeless black orbs which bobbled around on these little stems of nerves. I turned to run away and it swung it's arm at me, slicing into my jacket and back. Then, I heard another shotgun blast and watched as one of its claws blew into fragments of hard shell. This got it to focus on Dan and allowed me to double back into the room and find a place to hide. I slid into one of the cabinets on the floor while Dan fired another shot. This time, he missed it. The thing punched two swift holes into his abdomen and then flew off towards the bodies of Clark and the suited man. Dan screamed in pain and crawled towards the hole in the door.

"Don't come out, stay there and hide," he said. "Stay in there and..." he stopped crawling and that was it. I watched the blood pool around his stomach for a few minutes from the inside of the cabinet, but I knew he was dead. Saving my life was the only nice thing that Dan ever did for me.

But I loved that asshole.

I wish I could tell you that I grabbed the shotgun and finished the job, but that would be a lie. I'm still in this cabinet, hours later with my flashlight, a pen, and a notebook as the crabs continue to swarm. The only other things I've got on me right now is an empty bottle of Mountain Dew and the empty bottle of oxy that I crawled over to get from Dan's coat pocket.

I swallowed all of them about ten minutes ago.

I can hear the thing stomping its claws down onto the steel floor of the ship as it rips each crab hold open. The blue crabs are clicking back to it in a way I've never heard before in all of my years on the Bay.

They're talking to it.

Praising it.

I don't know if anyone will find us soon. Maybe the coast guard will show up and save the day. Maybe some other poor bastards will show up many years from now and find the golden box like we did. I really can't say, but I'm not going to be here to find out. I'm going to put this paper in the Mountain Dew bottle, seal it up, and toss it out into the ocean. If you're reading this right now, all I want you to do is find Abby Reynolds. She's only 3 right now, so wait until she's a little bit older. Then, I want you to find her and tell her about me. Tell her about her Daddy and how hard he tried. Tell her I found the true King of the Old Bay.

I hope she's proud of me.

ACKNOWLEDGMENTS

First and foremost: thank you Meg. Without you, I'd still be questioning myself and every single word in my rough drafts. Your feedback, support, and knowledge of the genre helped me get this thing done after years of neglect. For that, I will forever be grateful. I love you. To my Mom: thank you for all of your endless help and support as well. Thank you for editing the majority of my work. (The non-splattery stuff at least). Thank you to my Mom and Dad for letting me read Stephen King at age 7 and understanding that my love of horror was something to support and nurture instead of correct - even if it's not y'alls genre of choice. To Lilli: you can't read yet, but one day I look forward to hearing what you think. For now, yes, you can watch Gremlins. Shout out to Justin T. Coons for the phenomenal cover art. It was a dream come true to work with you and I hope to do it again someday soon.

Thank you to Sadie Hartmann for believing in me and helping me forge a path in this industry, no matter what road I'm traveling down. Cheers to the Night Worms crew. I love you all. Thank you to Andrew Fowlow for helping promote The Old Bay King (in addition to being a stalwart pillar of the indie horror community). Shouts to Tobias Dean and Andrew McDonald. Hello, Janine Pipe. To Tracy Robinson: where's my vintage paperbacks? Just kidding - thank you so much for helping me with "Magic in the Hat."

If you left me a review, rating, or feedback online, thank you. Acknowledgements are a tricky thing to write. I'm a naturally anxious person, so I fear I will forget someone, somehow. Just know that if you've supported me in anyway since I started this journey in 2018, I truly won't ever forget it. It means everything to me.

I've just begun to dig.

Until the next one,

Cheers!

-Donnie 4/20/21

The Razorblades in my Head

Although it's the first story in my collection, I took my time with this one. I wanted to set things off with a piece that's personal, memorable, and gross. To me, this story is a metaphor for creating and/or consuming horror. We love the horror genre for so many personal reasons, but true catharsis is something that I think we're all chasing in some shape or form. Horror often asks us to tackle the things that have scarred us in the past and I'm guessing that most of us have a "Bruce."

Fuck Bruce.

Third Grade

This story started as an exercise in writing the voice of a child. It was originally a harmless semi-autobiographical flash fiction piece. The following things are true: I had a best friend named Alex who moved to Maine. My class hamster was squished and killed (accidentally). I wrote a story called Blood Beach 2 and wrote song lyrics inspired by Nirvana. My teachers did not like me reading Stephen King.

The rest?

Well, that's up to you to decide what's fact and what's fiction, but I eventually revised this story to add what I assume my teachers thought would happen if they were to let a third grader read "adult" horror.

This story is my middle finger to them.

Stargazing

The concept of non-friendly extraterrestrial beings terrifies me. It's one of the only subgenres that inspires true fear in me. I've always wanted to tell an invasion story. I decided to write it in present tense to try and capture the sense of confusion and anxiety that an event like that would likely cause. I took inspiration from Paul Tremblay's SURVIVOR SONG in this regard. I've read or watched so many documentaries, films, and novels about this subject. Whether HG Wells or Whitley Strieber. I can't imagine something more horrific than the arrival of an advanced civilization that arrives to annihilate us or harvest our proteins / resources. At the same time, it's a metaphor for the history of humanity.

Gobble, Gobble

I credit the Gabino Iglesias open call for the "Halldark Horror" anthology as the jumping off point for this collection. I had been working on various projects for years that never came to fruition and I really wanted to get something done for that project. Sadly, I didn't meet the word count or deadline, but I did get this story out of it *and* the motivation to continue writing.

So, thank you, Gabino!

I wanted to write a story about the employees of a slaughterhouse getting eaten alive by Turkeys and it's really that simple. I wrote it 2 days after Thanksgiving. I loathe factory farming. This is a theme I will return to, frequently.

Magic in the Hat

I wrote this story for an open submission for a winter themed horror anthology. It was accepted, so be on the lookout for SERVED COLD, a charity anthology that is being put together by Regina St. Claire and the Booktube community in late 2021 / early 2022. After reading CLOWN IN A CORNFIELD, by Adam Cesare, I wanted to try my hand at writing teens. I have taught high school for 12 years and felt like it would be fun. I started with the simple concept of rebellious kids getting their comeuppance, but ended up with a story about friendship dynamics and the hardship of growing apart. I was also left with a fantastic setting for future horror stories (Greenfields) and an evil magician that used to work for a circus that will be fun to explore in the future.

It's Not Always Why

This was the final story I completed for this collection and the idea just sort of materialized one day while I was working on another piece. I honestly don't have the answers for this one. I think that's an okay position to be in as a writer.

Cosmic horror, baby!

The Stranger in the Squared Circle

I love professional wrestling. I honestly believe that it is the last bastion of true performance art in modern culture. Laugh if you want, but horror and pro-wrestling cultures crossover in many obvious *and* not so obvious ways. I have a whole universe in mind for what this story kicks off. I think a fictional league of monsters wrestling would be amazing. Google Chikara. I want to write a world like that, but they're not masked wrestlers, they're actual monsters. This story took me a long time to finish. I started it right before COVID emerged and got stuck with the pacing. I think this one helped me learn a lot about the short story format. I ended up deleting a few different scenes that tightened up the narrative and helped me realize that you don't always need a moment to moment recap of the action. Things can happen off the page. At 6000 words, this is the longest story in the collection. After THE RAZORBLADES IN MY HEAD, my next goal as a writer will be to tackle a single story with a word count of 15 - 30K words!

Toasted

This is a flash fiction piece I wrote for an anthology that was sadly cancelled before publication in late 2019. It is one of the first pieces I wrote after I made a promise to start taking writing seriously and it will likely end up as a much longer story one day.

For now, it's the classic story of a person who talks to their toaster. In the future, more will be revealed with how it got this way. Is the toaster actually talking?

That, I will not answer...yet.

Teddy

I've always loved how Brian Keene centered EARTH-WORM GODS (an all time favorite novel, for me) around Teddy, its elderly protagonist. There are far too few stories that feature main characters above the age of 65. I had such a strong picture for this character in my head: a lonely old man who decides to keep a cursed Teddy bear just to have someone around to talk to. That's really what this one is all about: loneliness.

However, I also dug the idea of a secret society of paranormal cremators. This concept was also inspired by Keene - his work is full of magicians that protect humanity. I've always loved the idea that our world is constantly being saved by forces that operate in secret. The order I mention will definitely make appearances in future stories. In fact, this will not be the last appearance of Wallace, Teddy, or Benton Fisk. Hell, we may even find out what happened to Beau some day.

A Bloody Heist

I love attempting to blend crime and horror together. Recently, I was thinking about heist movies (HEAT, ftw) when I thought it would be cool to tell a story about vampires who rob an armored truck for blood. It is short, but this may have been the most challenging story for me to write. I had to try and balance dropping hints for the reveal at the end, along with the present tense action of a heist. I'd love to adapt this into a short film or longer piece, one day.

Hourglass

This is the second major story set in the Greenfields gated community and it's just a ridiculous little satire about a cult of middle age men hoping to secure their golf clubs. It's also an adaptation of a film project I worked on and wrote in 2017.

I think it translated nicely to a short story. Some think of rural landscapes or urban jungles as the perfect backdrops for horror stories, but it is my belief that true horror is a gated community with a home-owners association.

The Old Bay King

I was stoned on a college couch in 2007 when I came up with the initial idea that became "The Old Bay King." This is the lesson for anyone out there doing anything creative: never give up on your ideas. I hate to think it will take me nearly 15 years for my next output, but you know what? I got this one done. Let me have this moment.

In all seriousness, I liked the idea of people on the ocean finding a ghost ship with a golden box on it. That was the original idea. The setup, contents of the box, and the ending shifted throughout the years. I'm happy with how it ended up. After reading Chesapeake Requiem, I figured out the final path of this one. The crabbing industry is notoriously challenging and faces a ton of threats due to climate change. I think that financial angst is something that drives a lot of my stories.

Would you take the box?

I probably would.

The following pages contain concept artwork for THE RAZORBLADES IN MY HEAD, created by Justin T. Coons and Luca Granai.

I am eternally grateful for their contributions to this project.

TEDDY

SKETCH

DenaM 2021

ABOUT THE AUTHOR

Donnie Goodman is a reader, writer, and collector of horror fiction. He runs the bookstagram page and YouTube show, "The Horror Hypothesis," and writes book reviews for SCREAM! Magazine. When he is not out in the wild searching for Paperbacks From Hell in Central Virginia, he is likely reading, writing, making music, or playing video games. THE RAZOR-BLADES IN MY HEAD is his debut. He also has some short stories coming soon from various publishers in the horror community.

instagram.com/thehorrorhypothesis

youtube.com/donniegoodman

twitter.com/donniegoodman_

facebook.com/donnie.hypothesis

Made in the USA
Middletown, DE
18 June 2021

42653173R00090